1000
CHEMISTRY QUIZ

Dr Maya Dube did her M.B.B.S from King George's Medical College, Lucknow, in 1946 and is the winner of many scholarships.

C. Dube is a prolific writer. He is an Honours graduate in the inter-disciplinary subject of Biological Chemistry from the University of Essex.

1000
CHEMISTRY QUIZ

Maya Dube
C. Dube

RUPA

Published by
Rupa Publications India Pvt. Ltd 1990
7/16, Ansari Road, Daryaganj
New Delhi 110002

Sales centres:
Allahabad Bengaluru Chennai
Hyderabad Jaipur Kathmandu
Kolkata Mumbai

ISBN: 978-81-716-7042-0

Eleventh impression 2014

20 19 18 17 16 15 14 13 12 11

The moral right of the author has been asserted.

Typeset by Mindways Design, New Delhi

To the memory of
Late Shrimati Gomti Trivedi
wife of Late Shri Raghunath Prasad Trivedi

PREFACE

I dived deep into the ocean and with the boat of my intellect rescued the precious, sunken jewel of true knowledge.

A treasure of knowledge lies hidden in the relatively young world of science. In our daily lives we come across problems and events that effect our existence and the quality of our life. We read from newspaper and magazine articles or books about the world around us, but never have had the time to think and ponder over them ourselves. To do so we need knowledge that is simple and readily available.

This is what this book is about. As you read, you will make an amazing discovery of facts about the wonderful world of chemistry: the birth of stars, journey into space, steel and plastics, diamonds and coal, the origin of petroleum, the earth and the universe. Facts and events centred around chemistry such as nuclear and chemical weapons, drugs, medicines, anaesthetics, fertilizers, cars, engines, turbo-jets, paints, explosives, foods, dyes, textiles and energy are included.

The book has been written for popularizing science. You do not need a degree in science or chemistry to read this book. *Anyone can read it.* The general reader as well as the chemist would be inclined to find in this book a unique approach that bridges the gap between a technical science and a general view of the world. It makes a seemingly high-brow matter look simple and readable. Even students of arts and social sciences, history and music, housewives and teachers can find a new field of interest and thought, of learning and quizzing.

Dr. **Maya Dube**
C. Dube

1000 CHEMISTRY QUIZ

Section 1

1. The spacecraft Pioneer-10, launched from earth, is hurtling away at great speed on a long voyage, out across Mars, Saturn and Pluto beyond the Solar system carrying a message that there is life on earth, in the hope that an alien civilization in an advanced stage of development may respond to this message. If you were asked to choose one of the following elements of matter, which one would best convey that there is life on earth?
   (a) Hydrogen (b) Carbon (c) Oxygen (d) Iron

2. The beautiful turquoise-blue Egyptian glaze of ceramic was an ancient technique of high quality, needing delicate control of temperature. This indicates, in those times, the possession of some knowledge of:
   (a) Blue chemicals (b) Ultramarines (c) Metallic compounds (d) Mercury

3. Our universe is very big, with millions of bright galaxies and stars that are much bigger than the sun and the earth. Do you know what is the universe made up of?
   (a) Oxygen (b) Hydrogen (c) Burning coal (d) Iron burning in a hot flame of oxygen

For answers see at the back

4. If you take a powerful telescope and study the light coming from distant stars and planets, you may sometimes come across substances mentioned here, whose presence shows that there may be life outside the earth. Can you pick the false one?

(a) Carbon monoxide (b) Carbon dioxide (c) Alcohol (d) Iron

5. Sometimes the engine of your car starts 'knocking'. To avoid this 'knocking', certain compounds are added to petrol. These are called anti-knocking agents. Can you tell which of the following is an anti-knocking agent?

(a) Tetraethyl lead (b) Carbon monoxide (c) White Petrol (d) Indole

6. Petroleum is a scarce natural resource which several countries are trying to explore on land and in oceans. We get so many things from petroleum, that is the starting point of many chemicals. Do you know that the origin of petroleum is in old:

(a) Earth (b) Fishes (c) Trees (d) Soft rock and clay

7. An organic compound must contain:

(a) Oxygen (b) Hydrogen (c) Carbon (d) Silicon

8. Gold and silver are called noble metals because:
(a) They are worn by noblemen (b) Ladies of royalty wear them as jewellery (c) They do not, normally, react in their natural environment (d) Even acids cannot dissolve them without strong heat

9. Diamonds are forever. Their beauty adorns crowns and jewellery of royalty and richness. Diamonds are made of:
(a) Pure sunlight (b) Pure, shining glass (c) Pure carbon (d) Pure beryllium

10. Sumerians and Babylonians were skilled metal-workers. They made coloured glasses and enamels. However, the making of transparent glass began:
(a) In 1000 A.D. (b) When Alexander the Great was born (c) In 500 B.C. (d) In 1,500 B.C.

11. Living things contain carbon in two forms, carbon-12 which is stable and carbon-13 that decays and declines in proportionate quantity. The technique that uses this principle for determining the age of fossils, skeletons, old trees and dinosaurs is known as:
(a) Carbon-12 dating (b) Radio-carbon dating (c) Fossil carbon (d) The Carbon Age

12. The curvature of optical telescopes gradually changes with the passage of time, because:
(a) They become out of focus (b) Of the heavy mechanical construction (c) Glass is a highly viscous liquid (d) Light from the stars has a bending effect

13. Who was awarded the Nobel Prize twice, once for Chemistry and once for Peace?
(a) Albert Einstein (b) Linus Pauling (c) George Wald (d) Wolfgang Pauli

14. Have you wondered how we can go back in the past by reversing all the processes in the world? Which branch of physical chemistry tells you about reversible and irreversible processes?
(a) Inorganic chemistry (b) Stereochemistry (c) Thermodynamics (d) Radioactivity

15. When a gas is compressed, its volume decreases. Who discovered through scientific experiments the quantitative relation between the pressure and volume of gases?
(a) Sir Isaac Newton (b) Sir Albert Einstein (c) Sir Thomas Roe (d) Sir Robert Boyle

16. Heat and electricity are different forms of energy. If a man eats food and burns it up, using 2,500 calories of energy in a day, then the power he produces is equivalent to lighting up a:

(a) 25 watt bulb (b) 56 watt bulb (c) 121 watt bulb (d) 500 watt bulb

17. Books, magazines, periodicals, greeting cards and calendars are printed in large numbers. Type-metal is used in printing presses as a picture, number or alphabet letter-type for printing. It contains:
(a) Oxygen (b) Lead (c) Chromium (d) Steel

18. Atoms are very small. We cannot see them with the naked eye. Even under the power of the optical microscope we cannot see them. What is their size (length) in comparison to that of man?
(a) Like an elephant on the earth (b) Like a fly and a whale (c) Like a flag on a mountain (d) Like an ant on the earth

19. Electric joints in electric circuits of radios, televisions, tape-recorders and related equipment are soldered, using solder which is made of:
(a) Iron and copper (b) Tin and lead (c) Lead and aluminium (d) Aluminium and copper

20. In ancient times, man was a 'nomad' (wanderer). Slowly, with the passage of time he learnt many things. He learnt to use metals. He began to use copper metal around:

(a) A.D. 1000 (b) 1000 B.C. (c) 2000 B.C.
(d) 4000 B.C

21. Think of dividing a piece of ice into half.
Divide it further and keep on dividing it
many times. The smallest piece of water
that you can get by this division is called:
(a) An atom (b) A particle (c) A molecule
(d) A crystal

22. The King of Bavaria (Germany) asked
Count Rumford to supervise the boring of
a cannon. Count Rumford was impressed
by the heat generated by friction and
suggested that it was created by the:
(a) Expenditure of power (b) Expenditure
of mechanical energy (c) Sparks of fire
(d) Fine turnings in the cannon metal

23. Which of the following is an artificial
element made by man?
(a) Helium (b) Iron (c) Gallium
(d) Americium

24. Different food sources, like lentils, milk
and soyabean contain different proteins.
Milk contains a Class I protein that is good
for health, namely:
(a) Casein (b) Caffeine (c) Calciferol
(d) Keratin

25. "Take seven parts of saltpetre, five of
young hazelwood (as charcoal) and five of
sulphur and so you will make thunder and

lightning." What was Roger Bacon describing in the year A.D. 1248?
(a) Desalination of water (b) Making of gunpowder (c) Electric discharge (d) Lightning conductor for underground earthing

26. Nature manifests its patterns and order in diverse ways, from the giant, revolving galaxies in the heavens to the beautiful, geometric forms of snow crystals that cover the earth, down to the elementary particles. The chemical properties of the elements of matter have been found to repeat in regular patterns. This pattern can be seen in the arrangement of atoms in the:
(a) Periodic table (b) Calculus table (c) Nutrition table (d) Chemical table

27. Nowadays, we hear the words 'acid test' and 'litmus test', used even in the social sciences. Do you know what happens to the colour of litmus paper when you put a drop of acid?
(a) From blue it turns red (b) From red it turns blue (c) It gets destroyed (d) It is unaffected by acid

28. Liquids flow from a higher to a lower level. Which liquid can climb up the walls of the glass vessel in which it is kept?
(a) Water (b) Alcohol (c) Liquid helium (d) Liquid nitrogen

29. Scientists who study and make observations in the field of thermodynamics say, that the total amount of energy in the universe is fixed, but:
(a) Matter is increasing (b) Disorder is increasing (c) Light is increasing (d) Gravitation is decreasing

30. Dyes are used for colouring various materials, like, cloth and plastic. William Perkins, the English Chemist, discovered dyes for colouring from:
(a) Baking ovens (b) Coal tar (c) Asphalt (d) Zinc

31. There are thousands of different organic compounds widely distributed in nature in diverse forms; in flowers, in plants, in grasses, in animals, in fishes, in petroleum and coal. Some have been synthesized by man. The most abundant organic compound in the world is:
(a) Methane (b) Alkaloids (c) Cellulose (d) Chlorophyll

32. Julius Robert Mayer wanted to see the world. So he sailed on the ship, *Java*, as a doctor in 1840. He found that the colour of blood of sailors was redder in the tropics. This observation led to a great contribution to science. What was his discovery?
(a) That heat and work are different (b) Heat and work are interchangeable, but their total energy is unchanged (c) That

the redder colour of blood was due to lesser consumption of oxygen in hot countries (d) More oxygen is consumed in colder countries

33. The nuclear process that takes place when a hydrogen bomb is exploded is of the same nature as the process:
(a) In the earth's centre (b) On the rings of Saturn and on its planets (c) In the sun and stars (d) During a red dust storm

34. Volcanoes erupt and spew molten rocks (lava) and hot gases. Earthquakes shake the earth. These natural phenomena have their origin in the belly (or deeper layers) of the earth. One important source of their energy is thought to be:
(a) Hot, molten steam trapped in the earth (b) The petroleum deposits stored under pressure (c) The pressure of ice at the earth's poles (d) Decay of radioactive matter in the earth

35. Turbo-jets move at high speed, generating tremendous heat which can melt ordinary metals. Which of the following is used for withstanding such high temperatures?
(a) High-nickel alloy (b) High-carbon steel (c) Chrome steel (d) Lead alloy

36. Hormones secreted by the body control growth, digestion, emotions, like anger and fear and perform many other functions.

The first hormone was artificially prepared in 1953 for which a Nobel Prize was awarded to:
(a) Linus Pauling in 1970 (b) Vincent du Vigneaud in 1955 (c) Frederick Sanger in 1960 (d) James Watson in 1965.

37. Fermentation of cider, wine or malt produces vinegar, which is used for preserving onions in pickles and in flavouring food. It is, essentially:
(a) Sodium carbonate (b) Acetic acid (c) Citric acid (d) Lime in soda

38. Electric cranes use powerful magnets for lifting heavy loads of steel in factories and stockyards by the power of magnetic attraction. These magnets lose their magnetism, when they are switched off, so that they can unload the freight. These magnets are, therefore, made of:
(a) Steel having a low carbon content (b) Iron alloy (c) Pig iron with high carbon content (d) Wrought iron, which has almost no carbon

39. Tungsten and Vanadium are important metals. When added to steel, they make it hard. Such steel alloys are used for making:
(a) Diamond safes (b) Forging presses (c) High-speed tools (d) Ball bearings

40. In some places a hard, cement concrete structure with pores is desired. Such a concrete can be made in the same way as baked bread having pores. The concrete pores can be made by the release of oxygen gas from inside the concrete by:
(a) Sodium peroxide (b) Hydrogen peroxide (c) Steam (d) Ozone

41. From methyl alcohol we get:
(a) The plastic perspex (b) The rubber neoprene (c) Bakelite, a hard plastic (d) Sponge rubber

42. When a nutrient like a fertilizer is present in large quantities in a pond, plants grow and decay in large numbers, suffocating the pond by not leaving sufficient oxygen in the water for supporting life. This kind of pollution is known as:
(a) Environmental pollution (b) Eutrophication (c) Smog (d) Greenhouse effect

43. Combs, toys, bowls, mugs and many items can be made from a plastic polymer mentioned here. Can you identify it ?
(a) Polystyrene (b) Metallic polysulphides (c) Teflon (d) Polyurethane

44. In the Periodic table, neighbouring elements are generally, more related to each other in their physical and chemical properties than the ones further away. Some families of related elements are

mentioned here. Can you pick the false one?
(a) Chromium, molybdenum and tungsten (b) Chlorine, bromine and iodine (c) Iron, cobalt and nickel (d) Oxygen, ca)on and phosphorous

45. Spacecraft returning from their voyage in outer space enter the earth's atmosphere with great speed, which makes them burning hot. Which metal is used as a shield to withstand these high temperatures?
(a) Iron (b) Titanium (c) Lead (d) Nickel

46. The hard-hitting shock waves released by the explosion of dynamite can travel at the high speed of:
(a) 100 m.p.h. (b) At the speed of sound, 700 m.p.h. (c) 1,800 m.p.h. that is 2.5 times the speed of sound (d) 18,000 m.p.h., that is, 25 times the speed of sound

47. The discovery of the fact that oxygen and hydrogen combine to form water, was a major step in the development of science. Who made this discovery?
(a) Joseph Priestley (b) Isaac Newton (c) Carl Wilhelm Scheele (d) Henry Cavendish

48. Calcium plays an important role in plants. It is a part of:
(a) Walls in plant cells (b) Plant protein (c) Nucleoproteins (d) Plant hormones

12

49. Every few years, a comet makes a dramatic appearance near the earth, with its tail glowing and extending across the sky. Comets consist of:
(a) Burning hydrogen gas (b) Rock and dust held together by ice (c) Yellow sulphur dust in red iron ore (d) Fluorescent mercury compounds in clay particles

50. Nylon is a well-known polymer used in fabrics and motor tyres. Nylon-66 is made from hexamethylene tetramine (having six methyl groups) and:
(a) Sulphur hexafluoride with six fluorine atoms (b) Sulphurous acid with six atoms of various elements (c) Adipic acid, a six-carbon chain fatty acid (d) Cobalt hexamine cation with six ammonia ligands

51. Gypsum is a widely occuring mineral. It is the sulphate of calcium with two molecules of water attached. On heating, it loses three quarters of its water and becomes:
(a) A pearl (b) Plaster of Paris (c) Baking soda (d) An ultramarine

52. Washing soaps are potassium and sodium salts of:
(a) Oleic, palmitic and stearic acids (b) Formic, acetic and maleic acids (c) Acetones, ketones and quinones (d) Sulphur, chlorine and fluorine

53. The earth is physically a habitable place being neither very hot nor very cold. Other planets may be very hot or very cold making it difficult for forms of life to survive. Venus has a surface temperature of:
(a) −100°C (b) Severe winter conditions in Siberia (c) Molten wax (d) Molten lead

54. Supersonic planes move at the speed of one-fifth of a mile per second. A body moving faster, at a speed of seven miles per second, can escape from the earth's gravitational pull into space. How fast are molecules of hydrogen moving at room temperature?
(a) One mile per second (b) Ten miles per second (c) At the speed of a supersonic jet (d) At the speed of light

55. Stainless steel is an alloy of chromium and nickel used in domestic utensils and in industry. It does not rust because:
(a) Nickel does not rust (b) Chromium forms a coating of oxide that protects iron (c) Iron forms an hard chemical with chromium (d) The carbon of steel combines with chromium

56. A molecule of water has the same shape as a molecule of:
(a) Chlorine oxide (b) Carbon dioxide (c) Boron fluoride (d) Acetylene

57. When light is absorbed a photochemical change may take place. When molecules are excited by a striking quantum (unit) of light:
(a) All of them react (b) None of them react (c) They may react in any number (d) A certain proportion of them react

58. Nowadays, several countries are generating electricity using nuclear raw materials. Dangerous by-products arise when energy is generated in a nuclear reactor. How many years would it take for the radioactive waste products of a light water nuclear reactor to, practically, lose their deadly radiation?
(a) 5 years (b) 50 years (c) 700 years (d) A million years

59. Tube-lights (or fluorescent lights) illuminate homes, signboards, shops and cities. Fluorescent light is emitted when electrons strike the coating of material on the:
(a) End of the light-tube (b) Outer surface of the light-tube (c) Inner surface of the light-tube (d) Metal part of the tube-light

60. Antibiotics fight disease, thereby, saving and preserving life. Which of the following is not an antibiotic?
(a) Tetracycline (b) Cyclohexane (c) Neomycin (d) Carbomycin

61. Bees select special flowers in jungles and gardens for collecting honey. The sugar contained in honey is:
(a) Glucose (b) Sucrose (c) Fructose (d) Maltose

62. Millions of dollars are spent in various countries in the treatment of wastes, by trying to remove the pollutants contained in them. Phosphate ions from fertilizers are sometimes present as contaminants in municipal sewage. These have been removed with some success by:
(a) Filtration (b) Heating at $70°C$ (c) Passing of chlorine (d) Passing of steam

63. Iron is used in different forms, like, cast iron, steel and alloys. The iron-carbon diagram is the basis for the branch of science known as:
(a) Carbon metallurgy (b) Stereochemistry (c) Ferrous metallurgy (d) Organic chemistry

64. Humus, a soil-enricher, is formed halfway in the process of decay of plants and animals. It contains the substances mentioned here. Can you pick the false one?
(a) 30% proteins (b) Lignins (c) Fats (d) Polyuronides (complex sugars)

65. It is said that in the early part of the eighth century A.D., the Greeks defeated the Persians by throwing a fireball invented by

Heliopolis. This fireball was a mixture of substances mentioned here. Can you pick the false one?
(a) Liquid bitumen (naphtha) (b) Phosphorous (c) Sulphur (d) Pitch

66. An increase in the number or size of dust particles in the air can lead to a decrease in the global temperature because these particles:
(a) Are very cold (b) Scatter blue light only (c) Can scatter all kinds of light (d) Increase moisture in the air

67. Some paint materials were known even in ancient times. Which of the following paints was used by the ancient Greeks?
(a) Zinc oxide (b) White lead (c) Alkyds (d) Latex paint

68. Which scientist discovered that the same amount of space was occupied by equal numbers of molecules of gases, irrespective of whether it was hydrogen or chlorine or fluorine?
(a) Marconi of Italy (b) Avogadro of Italy (c) Gay-Lussac of France (d) Wohler of Germany

69. When magnesium metal is combined with aluminium, zinc, copper and manganese, we get a light, hard alloy called electrum, which is used for making:

(a) Propellers of engines and aircraft
(b) Pressure cookers (c) Plates for light ships (d) Weights for measuring gold

70. Millions of dollars have been spent on research in Europe, U.S.A. and U.S.S.R. to find a way to properly harness nuclear fusion energy on a commercial scale in an effort to solve the energy crisis. Which of the following is a major hurdle in this challenging task?
(a) Non-availability of specialized engineers and scientists (b) Purifying the raw material (c) Finding safe ways of disposing of the waste products (d) To maintain a high temperature for the reaction

71. Radio housings and kitchen appliance regulators of plastic material are often made by the method of compression-moulding of plastic raw material. In this method, the plastic enters the mould:
(a) By heating it (b) By applying pressure (c) Through heat and pressure (d) By a blast of hot steam

72. A worldwide problem is the erosion of agricultural soil which affects the fertility of land. The matter in soil that holds soil minerals together are certain gums. These gums are made of:
(a) Proteins (long-chain amino acids)
(b) Polysaccharides (long-chain sugars)
(c) Triglycerides (fats) (d) Rubber latex-like material

73. Atomic clocks can measure time very accurately. They are not affected by the movement of the earth or the sun. The measurement is based on the:
(a) Movement of atoms (b) Chemical reaction of atoms (c) Size of atoms (d) Vibration of atoms

74. A large formation of soldiers and horses appeared to be a single body from a distance, in the sun. With such visions in mind, the Greeks developed the idea that matter consists of:
(a) Small drops of water (b) Atoms that cannot be divided (c) A single universe (d) Particles that move on energy from the sun

75. Certain unripe fruits, like, green apples, plums and currants, contain:
(a) Sulphuric acid (b) Hydrochloric acid (c) Vinegar (d) Maleic acid

76. When one cannot see distant or near objects, a visit to the optician or the optometrist sometimes becomes necessary. Eyes are tested by dilating the pupils with a very dilute solution of the alkaloid:
(a) Ephedrine (b) Atropine (c) Amphetamine (d) Adrenaline

77. The molecules (smallest particles) in the vapour of aluminium chloride:

(a) Have no shape (b) Are round (c) Are each shaped like a plane triangle (d) Look like a collection of randomly broken bricks

78. It was believed in the old days when science and religion shared similar ideas that a vital force was required to make matter if it was related to substances of which living things are made. Wohler, the German chemist, set aside this belief when he made ammonium cyanate from:
(a) Inorganic materials (b) Dead tissues of plants (c) Sea water (d) Air and sand

79. Protein obtained from various food sources such as beans, lentils or milk is digested in living tissues in various stages. An enzyme which helps this digestion is:
(a) Urease (b) Sulfatase (c) Trypsin (d) Protease

80. Without water, iron will not rust at ordinary temperatures. Iron and oxygen may lie together for hundred of years without any chemical reaction taking place. The moment a drop of water is added rusting can begin. Water acts as a:
(a) Chain reactor (b) Wettening agent (c) Catalyst (d) Solvent

81. Bentonite, a clay of alumina-silica is dropped from aeroplanes in the form of a slurry with water for the purpose of:

(a) Fumigation of plants (b) Fertilizing the soil (c) Cooling the soil (d) Spreading water over fires

82. By mixing a known quantity of a radioactive-labelled chemical to the normal form of the chemical and then by measuring the decline in radioactivity for each unit quantity of the mixture, we can accurately find the concentration of the chemical in a solution or mixture with other substances. This is known as:
(a) Qualitative analysis (b) Isotopic dilution analysis (c) Radioactive technique (d) Mixed radioactive labelling

83. Large quantities of various metals are required every day. About 90% of metal consumed by the world is:
(a) Iron (b) Steel (c) Copper (d) Aluminium

84. When life began on earth around two billion years ago by chemical reactions between simple, ordinary matter, the earth was:
(a) Cold (b) Green (c) Hot (d) Flat

85. An 'aerosol' is a fine dispersion of:
(a) Grease in water (b) Tiny droplets of liquid in the air (c) Tiny air bubbles in water (d) Chalk particles and sand in water

86. We have heard of sterling coins and sterling character. Sterling silver is:
(a) A compound of silver and nickel (b) A solid solution of silver in copper (c) 99% pure silver (d) A solid solution of copper in silver

87. How did life begin on earth? It is said that life on earth started by chemical reaction between some compounds mentioned here. Can you pick the false one?
(a) Water (b) Hydrogen and Nitrogen (c) Calcium (d) Carbon monoxide and Carbon dioxide

88. Acidity or alkalinity of a soil affects the growth of plants. Which plant does not grow well in soil that is slightly acidic to moderately basic?
(a) Alfalfa (b) Barley (c) Azalea (d) Beet-sugar

89. Rubber is very soft. Therefore, it is vulcanised and used in tyres. Vulcanised rubber resists:
(a) Jerking movement (b) Cold temperatures (c) Drops of acid rain (d) Wear and tear due to friction

90. The sixth planet of the solar system is the huge planet Saturn. The beautiful, coloured rings of Saturn are, mainly, made of:

(a) Red dust particles in the air (b) Greenish clouds of chlorine and sulphur dust (c) Millions of rocks and chunks of ice (d) Reflection of light from tiny mirrors of silver compounds

91. Who among the following believed that matter was made of earth, water, fire and air?
(a) Newton (b) Kapila (c) Aristotle (d) Cavendish

92. Arsenic is toxic. Therefore its presence, if any, in a room has to be detected. Which of the following gases can detect arsenic by reacting with it?
(a) Hydrogen sulphide (b) Fluorine (c) Methane (d) Acetylene

93. Kieselguhr (or diatomaceous earth) is a siliceous material found in Germany and California. Some of its uses are mentioned here. Can you pick the false one?
(a) In making dynamite, an explosive (b) For insulation against sound and heat (c) As a filter medium (d) For baking of bread

94. Explosives are used for cutting through rocks and hills for making bridges, roads and dams and in ore-mining. The explosive power of dynamite comes from a large amount of gas being suddenly created which destroys anything in its way with

great force. One litre of dynamite can suddenly release gases enough to occupy a:

(a) Room 9 feet by 9 feet (b) Box 2 feet by 1 foot (c) Thousand-litre drum (d) A bath tub

95. The sun is constantly radiating energy in the form of light, most of which is wasted in space. Some of it comes to the earth and is stored by plants. In one second on earth:

(a) 5 million calories of solar energy are stored as carbohydrates (b) 50 million calories are stored as uranium (c) 100 million calories of heat is reflected from the polar ice caps (d) 1000 million calories of heat is stored in the water of seas and oceans

96. Technological civilization is based on structural materials, particularly iron, which is extracted from its ores by:
    (a) Melting in a huge vessel with clay
    (b) Smelting in a blast furnace with coke
    (c) Heating in a tank with charcoal
    (d) Heating in a blast of carbon monoxide

97. An electron in an atom can be identified by:
    (a) Four quantum numbers (b) Its spin (c) Charge (d) The path in which it is spinning

98. It is difficult for matter to travel at the speed of light. Travelling beyond that speed is forbidden by Einstein's theory of relativity. Scientists in the U.S.S.R. found that, unlike matter, shadows could move faster than the speed of light by:
(a) Measuring the shadow of clouds (b) Rotating at high speed a light source (c) Measuring the movement of shadows cast by revolving planets (d) Switching an electric torch on-and-off in the night

99. If a piece of zinc and a piece of copper are brought in contact, they will form a weak, electrical combination. This was stated by:
(a) Sir Humphrey Davy in 1812 (b) Michael Faraday in 1813 (c) Einstein in 1927 (d) Volta in medieval times

100. Baking powders release carbon dioxide on heating and the dough (wheat and water paste) rises to form a loaf of bread with many holes, created by the escaping gas. This happens because baking powders contain:
(a) Sodium nitrate (b) Sodium bicarbonate (c) Ammonia (d) Protein in vinegar

Section 2

101. Bleaching preparations for domestic use contain chlorine. These should never be mixed with ammonia for the reasons mentioned here. Can you pick the false one?

(a) Poisonous products may be formed (b) The products may be explosive and poisonous (c) The products may be explosive (d) The products may leave brown stains on cloth and paper

102. Orlon and Acrilan are fibres of well-known textile materials of the same name. They are copolymers of:
(a) Acrylonitrile and 2-vinylpyridine (b) Alcohol and ester (c) Styrene and butadiene (d) Methane and acetone

103. With a Polaroid camera a picture can be taken and developed in a minute's time in the camera itself at the picnic spot, house or park. The camera contains colour-sensitive layers and a small bag of alkali. These are set into action when the:
(a) Camera is clicked (b) Film passes through the pressure of rollers (c) Film warms up (d) Colour chemicals on the film separate through a screen

104. Pigments for paints and printing ink are prepared as colloidal solutions. This is done by:
(a) Soaking in cold water (b) Grinding in a colloidal mill (c) Rapid stirring (d) Melting at low pressure

105. The sun is continuously releasing nuclear energy in the form of radiation. This:

(a) Makes it heavier than the stars (b) Makes it lighter (c) Prevents it from collapsing under its own weight (d) Prevents light from other stars from reaching the sun

106. Highly polymerised resins, like Bakelite plastics are made from phenol and formaldehyde. They are used for making many things, some of which are mentioned here. Can you pick the false one?
(a) Combs and fountain pens (b) Gramophone records (c) Paints (d) Electrical fuses

107. A very small sub-atomic particle was passed through large tanks of water containing Cadmium. When two gamma-rays were produced and a neutron was captured by Cadmium, the existence of this particle was inferred. Can you tell which particle was it?
(a) The proton (b) The anti-neutrino (c) The neutron (d) The electron

108. From our knowledge of the structure of the atom, we are able to understand why ammonia reacts with hydrogen chloride. Some reasons are mentioned here. Can you pick the false one?
(a) Ammonia can give a pair of electrons (b) A proton (positively charged particle) in hydrogen chloride can accept an electron pair from ammonia (c) The nitrogen atom

of ammonia gains electrons (d) The chloride ion formed has a complete set of eight electrons

109. If your teeth start decaying, the dentist may advise you to have your teeth filled. Some substances that are used as dental fillings are mentioned here. Can you pick the false one?
(a) Zinc oxychloride (b) Sorel's cement (c) Gold (d) Zinc

110. Wulfenite is a yellow to red mineral with a waxy lustre that occurs in ores of lead. It is an important source of:
(a) The metal molybdenum (b) The non-metal sulphur (c) The gas radon (d) Organo-metallic compounds

111. Take a closed box in which a mixture of chemicals is reacting in the forward and backward directions, both. Then, according to Le Chatelier, if you try to increase either the temperature or the pressure of the box, the whole system of chemicals reacting inside, will, unitedly, choose to react in that direction in which:
(a) This change is welcomed (b) It adjusts to accommodate this change (c) It opposes this change (d) The whole system collapses or explodes

112. Copper, a metal known from ancient times, has many uses, some of which are mentioned here. Can you pick the false one?
(a) In electric motor coils (b) In brass utensils and bronze statues (c) As an alloy in high-speed drills (d) In taps and water connections

113. The waste, or slag, that comes out at the bottom of a blast furnace for making iron from its ore, is not thrown away. It is used for making:
(a) Plastics (b) Roads (c) Dental powder (d) Glass moulds

114. To solve the problem of looking bald, human hair wigs are worn, which are very expensive. Synthetic wigs are made from a copolymer of vinyl chloride and acrylonitrile, called:
(a) Polyacrylonitrile (b) Cellulose (c) Dynel (d) PVC (or polyvinyl chloride)

115. Clay is used for making bricks and flower pots. If the clay article is not dried before 'firing' in a kiln, there will be evaporation of water from the surface and the:
(a) Article will become hard (b) Article will become soft (c) Kiln fire will be put out by steam (d) Article will develop cracks

116. Various metals, apart from iron, are in great demand for specialized applications. Which metal is used for making armoured

steel for tanks, warships and domestic safes?

(a) Copper (b) Magnesium (c) Manganese (d) Aluminium

117. In 1973, a Nobel Prize was awarded to Ernest Otto Fischer of Germany and Geoffrey Wilkinson of Great Britain for their outstanding work on joining organic compounds with metallic compounds. This was done as a part of research on:

(a) Growth of vegetables in a cold climate (b) Controlling pollution from vehicles (c) Developing high-speed photographic films (d) Recycling of plastics for a longer shelf-life

118. If gold is added to glass, we get highly-valued:

(a) Diamonds (b) Gems (c) Ruby glass (d) Pearls

119. Sometimes, a piece of cloth is dipped in a dye solution to allow the dye to penetrate the fibre. The cloth is, then, taken out and the dye is 'fixed' on the cloth by making the dye insoluble in water by chemical treatment. This process is known as:

(a) Ingrain dyeing (b) Direct dyeing (c) Vat dyeing (d) Colouring

120. Until the end of the nineteenth century, it was not clear as to what happened when a substance was dissolved in water and as to

why water sometimes becomes a better conductor of electricity on adding some substances. A Nobel Prize was awarded in 1903 for the idea that chemicals dissolved in a solvent like water split into electrically-charged particles. The prize was awarded to:
(a) Svante Arrhenius of Sweden (b) Ruzicka of Switzerland (c) Hinshelwood of Great Britain (d) Paul Debye of Holland

121. Entropy is a measure of disorder. For perfect, crystalline substances at the coldest, imaginable temperature known as the zero degrees absolute, it is said that entropy becomes:
(a) Very low (b) Zero (c) Constant (d) Minus

122. Copper and silver jewellery tarnish in the presence of moisture and:
(a) Oxygen (b) Nitrogen (c) Sulphur compounds (d) Carbon dioxide

123. The sun is like a huge 'hydrogen bomb' which is continuously burning matter for billions of years, generating heat and light. An hydrogen bomb needs less than half a kilogram of matter to give it explosive force. How much matter is lost in the burning, exploding sun?
(a) One kilogram per day (b) Two tonnes in an hour (c) Three thousand tonnes in

a minute (d) Four million tonnes in a second

124. Which of the following elements is used as an antiseptic?
(a) Bromine (b) Iodine (c) Chlorine (d) Neon

125. Tubes for draining water when made of certain materials have tremendous advantages. They can be accurately laid in straight lines, are easy to install and are less expensive. One man can lay a one-mile long pipeline every day with the help of a laser-guided machine. The pipes are made of:
(a) Metals such as copper alloy or steel (b) The plastics, PVC or polyethylene (c) Waterproof fabrics (d) Paper, aluminium foil and cotton fabric

126. Cassiterite (tinstone) is the oxide of tin, displaying colours ranging from light yellow prisms to brown and black. It is an important source of tin that is found in the places mentioned here. Can you pick the false one?
(a) Malaysia (b) Mexico (c) Tasmania (d) Sumatra

127. The Bureau International de Recuperation (BIR) is a worldwide trade association representing many industries. At Singapore, on 16 May 1990, it held a con-

ference on recycling waste materials. Some of the facts highlighted by the conference are mentioned here. Can you pick the false one?
(a) The Asian continent leads in recycling of waste paper (b) 30% of the world's demand of copper is met by recycling of copper scrap (c) 500,000 motor cars are scrapped every week in the world to give steel, tin, lead, gold, silver and aluminium (d) India is far behind the countries who lead the world in recycling of waste materials

128. Strong electrolytes are substances that conduct electricity very well when dissolved in solvents. Debye and Huckel suggested that this was because, in solution, strong electrolytes get completely broken into:
(a) Charged particles that conduct electricity (b) Light and heat (c) Electrons (d) Salt and water that moves with the current

129. Washing soaps produce a scum with hard water and not much foam, because hard water contains:
(a) Many suspended particles (b) Many dissolved inorganic salts (c) Chalk and sulphur (d) Organic matter

130. Which of the following is not a natural dye of either vegetable or animal origin?

(a) Saffron (b) Indigo (c) Tyrian purple
(d) Azo dye

131. Calcium magnesium silicate is:
(a) Prussian blue (b) Litmus (c) Asbestos
(d) Slate

132. If light of any frequency is passed through a substance, it is scattered. This scattered radiation contains some light that has a different wavelength. This is known as the:
(a) Coolidge effect (b) Fluorescence
(c) Raman effect (d) Solar spectrum

133. 'Smog', which means 'smoke' plus 'fog', irritates eyes and the throat. Smog is mainly caused by pollutants from automobiles and industries, when they:
(a) Form a smoke ring (b) React photochemically, due to the effect of ultraviolet light (c) Hit a dense shower of snow flakes (d) React with oxygen in the air due to lightning electrical discharge from clouds

134. When different metals like zinc, iron or tin were dropped in dilute sulphuric acid, it was found that the same gas was evolved, which burned explosively in air. This gas was
(a) Chlorine (b) Ammonia (c) Oxygen
(d) Hydrogen

135. Which of the following compounds is used as a sedative (sleep-inducing substance)?
(a) Calcium Chloride (b) Potassium bromide (c) Alcohol (d) Phosphorous trichloride

136. Which of the following is a super-cooled liquid?
(a) Ice cream (b) Ammonia (c) Glass (d) Wood

137. Modern paint industries try to give the best possible results by taking care of even the finest problems relating to paint. Some well-recognized problems of paints are mentioned here. Can you pick the false one?
(a) Fettling (b) Foaming (c) Yellowing (d) Destruction by ultraviolet light

138. Pollutants like particles of smoke or dust in the air or water create environmental problems. The extent of pollution in the environment can be known by the quantity in which they are present, This is indicated in terms of 'ppm', which stands for:
(a) Purity per microgram (b) Pollutant presence measure (c) Parts per million (d) Particles per mole

139. Aluminium occurs abundantly in the earth's crust, in the form of aluminium silicates. Which of the following is not an alumino-silicate?

(a) Mica (b) Clay (c) Kaolin (China clay)
(d) Brookite

140. Chemical reactions take place by combining or separating various atoms to form new groups of atoms. Thus, the atom is of the greatest interest for knowing why these changes take place. The statements here tell you about the mysterious world of the tiny atom. Which one is false?
(a) The atom has a tiny, dense core (centre) called the nucleus (b) Most of the volume of the atom is empty space (c) The nucleus has a small negative, electrical charge (d) The electrons of the atom revolve around the nucleus

141. When X-rays are passed through a solution of ferrous sulphate, it is converted into ferric sulphate. This principle is used for measuring radiation emitted by radioactive substances in an instrument called the:
(a) Geiger-Muller counter (b) Dosimeter (c) Cloud chamber (d) Oscilloscope

142. When white phosphorous is heated, it is converted into red phosphorous. If you add a little iodine, the conversion is faster. Here, iodine acts as:
(a) A lubricant (b) An oxidizer (c) A catalyst (d) An heating agent

143. Methane gas is an organic fuel obtained from the sources mentioned here. Can you pick the false one?
(a) Natural gas (b) Molasses (c) Coal gas (d) Sewage

144. In a hot star, at a temperature of a billion degrees Kelvin, two helium nuclei may combine to form Beryllium. By successive captures of helium nuclei, the elements, carbon, oxygen, neon and magnesium may be formed. This is known as:
(a) Star burning (b) Helium capture (c) An element series (d) Helium burning

145. With the passage of time, articles and machines get contaminated with various substances. Unwanted deposits of metals can cause inefficiency and loss. 1,2-dibromoethane is added to prevent lead metal being deposited in:
(a) Metal-working lathe machines (b) Water pipes (c) Petrol engines (d) Electric heaters

146. Two Chinese-born American scientists, Lee and Yang were awarded the Nobel Prize in 1957 for the discovery that ordinary matter, which did not have a sense of touch, sight, smell, taste or hearing, had:
(a) Also no preference for action in a particular direction (b) Preference for a particular direction (c) Control over living matter (d) The same properties on all sides

147. The starting point for manufacture of the anaesthetic chloroform, is:
(a) Chlorine (b) Formic acid (c) Acetone
(d) Carbon tetrachloride

148. The oceans contain a treasure of minerals. On the sea-bed lie important metals, like, manganese, nickel, cobalt and iron in lumps as small as a drop of water or large as tomatoes. These are known as nodules and are thought to have been formed by:
(a) Physical sedimentation (b) Volcanic eruptions (c) Chemical sedimentation
(d) Meteorites falling from space

149. Sugar candies are very hard. In order to make them soft, a substance is added, that also has a slightly sweet taste. Can you identify it?
(a) Glycerine (b) Alcohol (c) Honey
(d) Jaggery

150. Which one of the following elements forms compounds that are all coloured?
(a) Iron (b) Aluminium (c) Magnesium
(d) Chromium

151. The world's largest supply of sulphur comes from deposits in a relatively pure form, from:
(a) U.S.S.R. (b) China (c) U.S.A. (d) India

152. The radiations emitted by radioactive isotopes of elements help us in tracing the

path of many substances involved in various series or chains of chemical reactions such as, those that go on in the digestion of food, metabolism of protein and synthesis of carbohydrates, in plants, animals or in places, like, research laboratories and industry. For this immensely beneficial contribution, a Nobel Prize was awarded in 1943 to:
(a) Alston of Great Britain (b) Sabatier of France (c) Adler of Germany (d) George de Hevsey

153. The 'Green Revolution' in agriculture was made possible by synthetic fertilizers. One of the most widely used nitrogen fertilisers is:
(a) Ammonium chloride (b) Sodium nitrate
(c) Ammonium sulphate (d) Nitroglycerine

154. When items of jewellery made of base metals like copper, iron or nickel are placed in a solution containing a compound of gold, a film of gold is deposited by:
(a) Heating (b)Adding acid (c) Cooling to 5 degrees centigrade (d) Passing an electric current

155. Zinc oxide is used in:
(a) Black glasses (b) White paint (c) Bleaching of paper (d) Sweet-smelling soaps

156. Nickel and cadmium are used in combination:
(a) In electric batteries having a very long life (b) In alloys that can resist high pressure (c) As a catalyst (d) In cooking utensils

157. A deficiency of insulin, an hormone, causes diabetes. Diabetic patients, therefore, take insulin injections to prevent an excess of sugar. For discovery of the chemical structure of insulin, using X-ray photography, a Nobel Prize was awarded in 1958 to:
(a) Frederick Sanger of Great Britain
(b) Staudinger of Germany (c) Virtanen of Finland (d) Sir Alexander Fleming

158. Graphite is used for making electrodes and articles like writing pencils. It is made by heating coke with some silica for many hours in:
(a) The presence of air (b) An high electric furnace (c) A blast furnace (d) A blast of steam under pressure

159. Beautiful crystals arise from various chemical substances. A single chemical can, sometimes, give rise to different crystals because of different:
(a) Composition (b) Arrangement of atoms in space (c) Angles of vision (d) Weight of atoms

160. The strength of steel greatly depends on how it is 'quenched'. This means that the:

(a) Steel is heated (b) Steel is forged (c) Hot steel is cooled (d) Steel is bent

161. In 1896, Henri Becquerel, a French chemist, by chance left some photographic films covered with a black paper near a sample of uranium. On developing the film, it was found to have been exposed. This led to the discovery of:
(a) Infrared rays (b) Plutonium (c) Radioactivity (d) Television transmission

162. Silicones are a variety of several polymers with unique properties. Some of their uses are mentioned here. Can you pick the false one?
(a) In lubrication at low temperatures (b) As electric condensers (c) In moulds for casting (d) In making synthetic yarn

163. Iron is a metal that is obtained in different forms. Which of the following is incorrect?
(a) Pig iron is impure (b) Cast iron can be cast into drain pipes (c) Wrought iron can be welded and forged (d) Pig iron is made from cast iron

164. When camphor is heated, it:
(a) Melts (b) Reacts (c) Sublimes (d) Boils

165. Niels Bohr became world famous when he created a theoretical picture of the atom based on the:

(a) Stars in the galaxy (b) Model of the planets revolving around the sun (c) Behaviour of waves in the ocean (d) Clouds in the sky that move and mix in changing shapes

166. Pollution of lakes and rivers affects aquatic life. Fish cannot live in water that has oxygen less than 4 milligrams per litre Other fresh water aquatic life (including anaerobic bacteria) also cannot survive without adequate oxygen. 'BOD' stands for:
(a) Basic oxygen decline (b) Bacterial oxygen depletion (c) Biological oxygen demand (d) Building oxygen depots

167. Fires have sometimes started when water has suddenly seeped into bags containing quicklime lying on the floor of a godown. The reason for this is that water reacts with quicklime:
(a) To form a corrosive acid (b) And liberates tremendous heat (c) And exerts pressure (d) And liberates inflammable gases

168. Sometimes water is contaminated with colouring material that is present as a pollutant from various sources of waste. Which of the following is not a common colour pollutant in water?

(a) Peat-like material (b) Hume-like material (c) Salts of calcium (d) Salts of iron and manganese

169. 'pH' is a measure of the acidity or alkalinity of a liquid such as a chemical solution, blood, water or a medium like soil. The term 'pH' comes from:
(a) Poue voir hydrogene (or hydrogen power) (b) Pure hydrogen (c) Hydrogen purity (d) Principle of hydrogen

170. Great advances were made in scientific and technological fields in Europe. By the year 1800 progress had been achieved in the use of material resources for the betterment of living and working conditions. Some landmarks are mentioned here. Can you pick the false one?
(a) Matches for lighting domestic fires were made of chlorates (b) The use of steel alongwith concrete was started for construction of buildings (c) Fabrics and clothes were bleached by chloride of lime (d) Gas was obtained from coal for domestic and industrial lighting

171. Viruses exist on the borderline between living and non-living matter. They cause diseases in animals, plants and human beings. They are made of biochemicals known as:
(a) Carbohydrates (b) Nucleoproteins (c) Enzymes (d) Peptones

172. Many bacteria are useful to plants. Autotrophic soil bacteria are useful to plants because they convert nitrogen from a less useful and toxic form to a readily available form. They convert:
(a) Nitrite to nitrate (b) Nitrate to nitrite (c) Nitrate to ammonium salts (d) Ammonium salts to nitrate

173. Pitchblende, the main ore of the radioactive elements, Uranium and Radium is found in the places mentioned here. Can you pick the false one?
(a) France (b) South Africa (c) Mexico (d) Finland

174. The odourless, poisonous gas mixed with smoke that arises from burning coal is:
(a) Carbon dioxide (b) Nitrogen (c) Carbon monoxide (d) Methane

175. *Rasarnava* was a treatise of the Tantric Saiva Cult in India. It mentioned:
(a) The names of various steels (b) Preparation of alcohol from barley (c) The different colours imparted by flames to metals (d) The growth of green plants in a nitrogen-rich soil

176. The air we breathe in modern times can no longer be said to be 'fresh'. With every breath that we take, we inhale billions of molecules of pollutant chemicals. Some man-made sources of pollution are men-

tioned here. Can you pick the least con-. trollable one?
(a) Motor cars and other vehicles
(b) Chemical and other industries
(c) Domestic cooking (d) Thermal power plants

177. Which of the following artificial substances is harder than diamond?
(a) Adamantane (b) Carborundum (silicon carbide) (c) Chrome steel (d) Borazon (boron nitride)

178. Bronze statues and articles of copper slowly tarnish in air and turn green. This green colour is due to the formation of:
(a) Copper sulphate (b) An oxalate
(c) Basic copper sulphate (d) Copper oxide

179. Chemical weapons have been developed which are poisons that interfere with the enzyme cholinesterase of the human nerves, glands, muscles and heart-beat leading to fatal consequences. Which of the following is a deadly nerve gas developed during the Second World War?
(a) Phosgene (b) Nitric oxide (c) Sarin (d) Argon

180. In the early part of the twentieth century, experiments were conducted using cathode-ray tubes which produced cathode-rays (or electron beams). These tubes were the forerunners of:

(a) Light arcs of cinema projectors (b) Picture-tubes of television today (c) The latest transistors (d) Modern lighting systems

181. When glass is heated, it:
(a) Melts only above 1000°C (b) It vapourises (c) It does not melt at a fixed temperature (d) It has a fixed melting point for each type of glass

182. Metals generally have high melting points. Even the compounds they form are often difficult to melt. However, the lowest melting point of matter that contains metal has been found to be as low as 185 degrees below the freezing point of water. Which is this metallic compound?
(a) Alum (b) Lithium tetramine (c) Magnesium sulphate (d) Sodium zirconate

183. It is sometimes essential or useful to know where a chemical can be obtained from for scientific, experimental or other essential purposes. Which of the following is incorrect?
(a) A hypo solution can be obtained from a photographic material store (b) Borax from a drug store (c) Quicklime from builders' supplies (d) Magnesium ribbon from a hardware store

184. Lawn tennis hard courts are sometimes made of flat slabs of shale. These slabs are bound by:

(a) Iron oxide (b) Hydrated calcium chloride (c) Feldspar (d) Argentite

185. The first dye that was prepared synthetically was:
(a) Malachite green (b) Azo-dyes (c) Mauveine (d) Phthalein dyes

186. According to Al-Beruni, the traveller, people in India in the eleventh century A.D. were familiar with some chemical processes and methods mentioned here. Can you pick the false one?
(a) Sublimation of solids (b) Calcination of substances (c) Distillation at low pressures (d) Chemical analysis

187. Nowadays, various plants are commonly grown in greenhouses. When the soil of these greenhouse nurseries is sterilized with methyl bromide gas, it leads to deficiency of the nutrient:
(a) Zinc in plants (b) Chlorophyll in green leaves (c) Cellulose in roots (d) Iron in red flowers

188. Out of the energy received from the sun every year, one-third is reflected back immediately into space. How much of it is absorbed by plants for photo-synthesis, from which we ultimately get a major part of our energy requirement in the form of coal, wood, petroleum or natural gas?

(a) Half (b) Quarter (c) One-fifth (d) One-tenth

189. Formaldehyde is used for making many things. Some are mentioned here. Can you pick the false one?
(a) Adhesives (b) Bakelite (c) White tooth-powders (d) RDX (or cyclonite), a powerful explosive

190. If a nuclear reaction is allowed to proceed unchecked it may lead to a mighty explosion. Therefore, when nuclear energy is intended to be harnessed for generation of electricity, potentially destructive neutrons released in a nuclear reaction are absorbed by some of the arrangements mentioned below. Can you pick the false one?
(a) A pile of bricks made of graphite
(b) Heavy water (c) Long rods of cadmium
(d) Cubical blocks of steel

191. The Atomists believed that matter was made of atoms that are solid and which could not be destroyed. To this school of thought belonged:
(a) Leucippus (500 B.C.) and Democritus (460 B.C.) (b) Galileo (c) Anaximander (611-545 B.C.) (d) Thales of Miletus (580 B.C.) and Empedocles of Sicily

192. The glass used in windows in buildings used to be a bulging hemisphere with a

'seeing-hole' in the centre for looking out of the windows. The windows were not plane (flat) since there were no glass sheets. The making of plate glass (flat sheets) started around:
(a) 100 years ago in the times of Bismarck
(b) 200 years ago in the period of Napoleon
(c) 300 years ago in Sweden (d) 400 years ago when Sir Thomas Roe came to India

193. The active portion of soils are the clays. These were thought to be small particles of minerals like quartz. X-ray and other studies have revealed the correct facts, which are mentioned here. Can you pick the false one?
(a) Clays are, mainly, in colloid or crystalline form (b) Clays have specific compositions (c) Clays do not include mica (d) Clays are reformed products of primary minerals, like, quartz

194. Common salt or table salt is part of our daily diet. However, it is also a basic raw material for many industries. Common salt is converted into important and useful industrial chemicals mentioned here. Can you pick the false one?
(a) Sodium peroxide (to make hydrogen peroxide) (b) Sodium sulphate (used in making glass) (c) Sodium nitrate (used in the fertilizer industry) (d) Sodium oxide (used in making paints)

195. The first Blast furnaces for making large quantities of iron are said to have been developed before the birth of Christ, in:
(a) China (b) Italy (c) Korea (d) Egypt

196. Polymers like plastics, rubber, nylon and filament yarn, are made of chemical constituents that can be imagined to be tiny:
(a) Rivers (b) Laces of bead (c) Gramophone discs (d) Bunches of sticky sweets

197. One of the most simple and brilliant ways of protecting iron is 'cathodic protection'. Iron is connected to a material that corrodes in preference to iron. Can you pick the false one?
(a) Natural gas pipelines are connected to zinc rods embedded in the ground (b) Oil pipelines are connected to zinc rods embedded in the earth (c) Iron windows are coated with white lead (d) Stand pipes are connected to rods of magnesium connected to the earth

198. In some parts of the world a primitive form of cultivation exists in which trees and forests are burnt and reduced to ashes. This ash is basic in its chemical properties and its presence in soil is just like the effect of:
(a) Adding urea to the soil (b) Removing oxygen from the soil (c) Adding lime to the soil (d) Cooling the soil

199. A lot of money is spent on preventing rusting of windows, bridges, poles, vessels and articles. Some of the ways in which steel can be prevented from rusting are mentioned here. Can you pick the false one?
(a) Painting (b) Electroplating or galvanizing (c) Pickling (d) Coating steel with plastic

200. The *Elements of Chemistry*, published in 1789 described elements with modern chemical names. It contributed significantly to the progress of chemistry. The book was written by:
(a) Lavoisier of France (b) Cavendish (c) Scheele (d) Mendeleev of Russia

Section 3

201. Peppermint, orange, lemon and ginger oils are used for flavouring food and sweets. They can be extracted from plant sources by using solvents, like:
(a) Alcohol (b) Ammonia (c) Water (d) Vinegar

202. The natural, agricultural resources of the world are limited. They cannot sustain a world population of more than 5 billion people. This large population has been supported by means of fertilizers. Therefore, it is true that this large population is today supported by Haber's process of:

(a) Making nitrogen (b) Making ammonia
(c) Photosynthesis (d) Making phosphate

203. The hard, plastic covers of telephones are made of polymers of:
(a) Phenol-formaldehyde (b) Acrylonitrile
(c) Styrene (d) Fluoromethane

204. Which of the following is a physical change?
(a) Burning of wood (b) Melting of steel
(c) Photosynthesis (d) Radioactive decay

205. Tin is a highly valued metal that occurs naturally in mineral ores like cassiterite (or tinstone). Some of the world's main suppliers of tin, having large deposits, are mentioned here. Can you pick the false one?
(a) Bolivia (b) Indonesia (c) Italy
(d) Malaysia

206. Detergents are made usually from products obtained by cracking of petroleum, like:
(a) The chloroalkanes (b) The sulphur compounds of benzene (c) The sulphide of hydrogen (d) Propylene derivatives

207. The basic chemical building block of natural rubber obtained from trees is:
(a) Isoprene (b) Vinyl chloride
(c) Acetylene (d) Neoprene

208. Human blood is composed of red cells, lipids and many chemicals. The pH (hydrogen ion concentration) of blood is maintained by carbon dioxide, carbonic acid in the body and chemical constituents of blood. This maintenance of the pH is known as:
(a) Colloidal action (b) Buffer action (c) Acidity (d) Salt balance

209. In actual practice, it is impossible to attain the lowest temperature known to scientific theory, namely, the zero degrees absolute. This is nothing but a simple statement of the third law of:
(a) Newton's theory of motion (b) Thermodynamics (c) Science (d) Cryogenics

210. Antibiotics help in curing disease by killing bacteria. Sulpha drugs, on the other hand, help by:
(a) Precipitating bacteria (b) Removing bacteria (c) Decreasing the size of bacteria (d) Stopping the growth of bacteria

211. Emperors tried to impress their guests with cutlery made from a metal which was considered more precious than gold a hundred years ago. What was this metal?
(a) Cobalt (b) Nickel (c) Chromium (d) Aluminium

212. Under the high pressure of sea water at great depths, nitrogen breathed can cause

pain in sea divers. Therefore, the oxygen in pressurized suits of divers is mixed with:
(a) Purified air (b) Helium (c) Argon (d) Hydrogen

213. A chemical bond between two atoms is:
(a) The link between them (b) The energy of the individual atoms (c) The tunnel in an atom through which the other one can pass (d) A third, connecting atom

214. Fluorine, chlorine, bromine, and iodine form a family of related elements, known as:
(a) Purines (b) Halogens (c) Light gases (d) The aromatic ring

215. When an agricultural or horticultural field is covered with plastic sheets, the temperature of the soil increases and helps plants to grow. On the Hawaii Islands, when sheets of black polythene were laid to cover the ground, the growth of pineapples increased by:
(a) 1% (b) 5% (c) 10% (d) 50%

216. Gold, a precious metal has many uses apart from making jewellery. Some of these are mentioned here. Can you pick the false one?
(a) In photography (b) For filling teeth cavities (c) Electroplating (d) In gem polishing

217. Mosaic flooring is made of marble chips embedded in cement. The floor, after the setting of the cement is made smooth by operating a machine that revolves at high speed black, hard blocks of:
(a) Carbon (b) Carborundum (silicon carbide) (c) Graphite (d) Hard slate

218. Coastal towns and places have their own problems. One of them is the effect of sea water on the articles installed or in use. Which of the following metals is least corroded by the chemical action of sea water?
(a) Zinc (b) Nickel (c) Iron (d) Cadmium

219. Alchemists were pseudo-scientists pursuing chemical phenomena in the old days of superstition. They, sincerely, believed that chemicals were gifted with human nature and that a chemical reaction took place when chemicals:
(a) Fought together (b) Loved each other
(c) Smiled on the dark side of the moon
(d) Formed social groups

220. Chromium-plated steel is a material of popular use. During its process of manufacture, the effluent contains chromate and cyanide ions as impurities. After these are chemically removed, carbon dioxide and salt (sodium chloride) still remain as impurities. This salt solution is

purified electrolytically by adding carbonaceous matter which acts as:
(a) A cathode (b) An electrode (c) As microcells (d) As a salt absorber

221. A new technique has been developed where a jet of water in admixture with hard, fine particles of abrasives is thrown at high speed for:
(a) Softening wood for furniture making (b) Polishing metal (c) Cleaning plastic sheets (d) Cutting steel

222. There is a big demand for phosphates. Which small island-nation has one of the world's biggest phosphate deposits, where it is said that the mining activity may be reducing its size?
(a) Japan (b) Phillipines (c) Mauritius (d) Nauru

223. After hair oil bottles has come the new trend of hair-sprays. Hair sprays generally contain resins in a volatile solvent. Upon drying, they leave a thin film that holds the hair in place. Which of the following is a resin used in hair spray?
(a) Polyvinyl pyrrolidone (PVP) (b) Polyvinyl alcohol (c) Polyester (d) Polythene

224. The engines of the rocket thàt helped the Apollo 11 spacecraft to land on the moon, used for rocket fuel power:

(a) Oxygen (b) Hydrogen (c) Hydrazine
(d) Propane

225. At sunset, if we look at the sun directly, it appears red in colour because:
(a) Blue light is scattered away (b) Red light is scattered away (c) Other colours are lost in the red glow (d) Red is the natural evening colour of the sun

226. Chlorine forms well-known compounds of great value, uses of some of which are mentioned here. Can you pick the false one?
(a) As solvents (b) As antiseptics (c) As anaesthetics (d) As cutting tools

227. Plastic sheet covers placed on the ground increase the temperature of the soil and help plants to survive in cold areas. In Alaska, plastic sheet covers help in:
(a) Early maturing of sweet corn (b) Growth of potatoes (c) Cultivation of roses (d) Planting ginger

228. Transition metals are hard and lustrous substances with high melting points and form highly coloured compounds. Which of the following are not transition metals?
(a) Chromium, cobalt and copper (b) Iron, manganese and nickel (c) Scandium, titanium, vanadium and zinc (d) Aluminium, lead and tin

229. An industrial plant, in which ore was smelted, released so much of sulphur dioxide that its effects were found 52 miles away on plants in the direction of the wind. Some effects are mentioned here. Can you pick the false one?
(a) Bleached or yellow spots on green leaves
(b) Decolourisation of the plant stem
(c) Decrease in the growth of plants
(d) Decrease in the number of plants per unit area

230. 'Koroseal' is a long, chain polymer. When mixed with plasticizers, it forms an excellent plastic. Some of its uses are mentioned here. Can you pick the false one?
(a) In wire and cable insulation (b) Lining material for tanks (c) For water-proofing (d) For sun-shading

231. Which of the following is an antibiotic used in the treatmant of typhoid fever?
(a) Heparin (b) Chloramphenicol (c) Sylvarsan (d) Quinine

232. Calcium carbide reacts with nitrogen to form a black mixture of carbon and cyanamide. This mixture, known as nitrolime, is used as:
(a) A paint (b) A dye (c) A fertilizer (d) An explosive

233. The neutron is a neutral (non-electrical) particle in the centre of the atom. It was

discovered when a tiny piece of the metal, beryllium, was bombarded with alpha particles. This discovery was made by:
(a) Niels Bohr (b) Rutherford (c) Chadwick (d) Enrico Fermi

234. In a mirror your right hand becomes the left one and vice-versa. In nature too, many compouds exist, which can have their opposites, that are their mirror-images. For example, sugars like glucose, fructose, and amino acids exist in nature in one of two possible mirror images. These mirror image compounds can be distinguished by:
(a) Their chemical reaction with sulphuric acid (b) Their melting point (c) The direction in which they rotate polarized light (d) The spectrum of white light

235. A nuclear submarine stays longer under water because it has a sustained fuel supply. In the early nuclear submarines, heat was transferred from the nuclear reaction chamber by:
(a) A graphite pile (b) Cadmium control rods (c) Molten sodium (d) Steel rods

236. The gas in a refrigerator causes cooling on expansion because:
(a) Work done by the gas is converted into heat (b) Heat of the gas is lost as work done by the gas (c) The density of heat goes down (d) The heat is spread over a larger space

237. X-ray studies have shown that coke, charcoal, lamp black are forms of carbon having the chemical structure found in graphite. The 'carbon' of microphones in public address systems use:
(a) Coal (b) Lamp black (c) Graphite (d) Charcoal

238. Coffee stains on clothing, paper, plastic or crockery and trays can be properly removed by:
(a) Sodium hypochlorite (b) Water (c) Vegetable oil (d) Vinegar

239. Plastics are:
(a) Polymers (b) Acids (c) Salts (d) Solvents

240. Physical and chemical processes in a fresh water ecological system like a lake, and their effect on plants, fishes and other forms of aquatic life are studied by scientists. This study is known as:
(a) Fresh water science (b) Limnology (c) Palaeology (d) Water Ecology

241. A substance can be identified because its chemical environment often shows up like a finger print in a spectrum. This fine region of finger prints of the chemical environment of a chemical compound is created by:
(a) Nuclear magnetic resonance (b) Ultraviolet light (c) Infrared radiation (d) X-rays

242. When a metal is heated in a flame, the electrons absorb energy and jump to a higher, excited state of energy. When they fall back to the lower energy state, they emit light, which we see in:
(a) An absorption spectrum (b) An emission spectrum (c) The Raman spectrum (d) Fluorescence

243. Dacron is an excellent cloth which is resistant to wrinkles and moth. It is a synthetic polyester fibre made from:
(a) Terephthalic acid and ethylene glycol (b) Caprolactam and alcohol (c) Vinyl pyridine (d) Phthalic acid and cellulose

244. Serving trays for tea or food, made of aluminium, often have coloured finishes. These finishes are formed when an electric current is passed, which creates an oxide of aluminium layer that absorbs dyes. This is called:
(a) Sherardizing (b) Anodizing (c) Galvanizing (d) Annealing

245. An ore is a mineral from which a metal can be extracted:
(a) By chemicals (b) By melting (c) Profitably (d) Scientifically

246. In plants like peas, bacteria are known for their ability to 'fix' nitrogen from:
(a) Air (b) Water (c) Soil (d) Fertilizer

247. Starch is made by photosynthesis in the leaves of plants. It is found in rice, potatoes and many vegetable sources. It can be detected with a drop of iodine. In the presence of starch, iodine:
(a) Decolourises (b) Turns blue
(c) Vapourises (d) Turns into a black solid

248. When polyester resins are added to fibre glass, it becomes strong. Some applications of polyester resins are mentioned here. Can you pick the false one?
(a) In boat-hulls (b) In glazing of aeroplanes (c) In sky ventilators (d) In brake linings

249. A good amount of evidence is there to indicate that stars make heavy elements like the ones found on earth. Light coming from a star was collected through a telescope. If showed that an element was present in the star, whose half-life span was much less than the age of the star, which showed that it was made much after the star was born. Which of the following elements was this?
(a) Uranium (b) Technetium (c) Polonium
(d) Radium

250. From formaldehyde we get formalin, which is a powerful:
(a) Painkiller (b) Bleaching and whitening agent (c) Preservative and disinfectant
(d) Deodourant

251. A typical battery used is the mercury cell, which is used in:
(a) Radio transistors (b) Television sets
(c) Electric watches (d) Electric torches

252. Graphite is used in pencils. It leaves a black trace of writing on paper because it consists of layers of carbon atoms that:
(a) Fall easily (b) Are attracted by paper material (c) Are wound inside, like a long thread (d) Slide over each other

253. Salicylic acid, picric acid, aspirin, nylon and plastics have a common raw material, namely:
(a) Methane (b) Formic acid (c) Phenol
(d) Alcohol

254. In the year 1908, a great explosion took place in Tungska, Siberia, which was heard for miles. Forest fires broke out and trees were flattened in a circle. But the trees in the centre stood straight. It is believed, with striking evidence, that this mysterious event was due to:
(a) The bursting of an oil well (b) Lightning and thunder (c) The explosion of a nuclear ship from outer space (d) Explosion of a large deposit of uranium in the earth

255. Various materials are being tried as sources of fuel for motor cars. Experiments conducted in France have shown that energy could be obtained for motor cars from:

(a) Jerusalem artichokes (b) Potatoes
(c) Vinegar (d) Lime

256. Gold is often found near a well-known mineral mentioned here. Can you find it?
(a) Mica (b) Quartz (c) Feldspar (d) Galena

257. If water samples are taken from the sea, rivers, clouds, lakes or snow, they will be found to contain hydrogen and oxygen in the ratio of 1:9 This clearly demonstrates the law of:
(a) Combining volumes (b) Definite proportions (c) Chemical equilibrium (d) The relation of elements in the periodic table.

258. Thin metal foils are commonly used in food and cigarette wrapping, in food and art decoration and in electrical contacts. Which of the following is/are not used as a foil?
(a) Aluminium (b) Silver and gold (c) Tin and copper (d) Lithium and zinc

259. During A.D. 1100 to A.D. 1300, known as the Tantric Period of chemistry in India, preparations of mercury were used for:
(a) Temperature measurement (b) Curing disease (c) Weighing gold (d) Polishing wood

260. Which of the following liquids does not dissolve in water?

(a) Alcohol (b) Ammonia (c) Kerosene
(d) Acetic acid

261. In rocky, mountainous places it was observed that fertilizers did not affect the production of plants where the land was already fertile. Which one of these is expected to be fertile?
(a) Soil formed from granite rock (b) Red soil (c) Soils from basic, igneous rocks (d) Soil on steep slopes

262. One of the aims of the car-making industry is to have streamlined, shining cars that look better on the road. Car bumpers have a shiny, protective metallic coating that is made of:
(a) Tin (b) Chromium (c) Aluminium (d) Silver

263. For comparing the results of scientific experiments conducted in thousands of chemical laboratories dotted all over the world, a common scale for measuring time, length and mass is necessary. The standard kilogram is accepted as the mass of matter contained in a piece of:
(a) Platinum kept at Sevres (France) (b) Gold kept at Uppsala (Sweden) (c) Lead at Warsaw (Poland) (d) A diamond kept at Oslo (Norway)

264. Coking coal is used for making iron. It was invented by Abraham Darby of England

when he added to coal the right proportion of:

(a) Lime (b) Steam (c) Sulphur (d) Copper

265. With a world-wide increase in demand and consumption of goods, there is a shortage of plastics, newsprint and many materials. This has caused a re-thinking for conserving materials by re-cycling. Where have laws been passed, making it compulsory for citizens to segregate waste into 'paper', 'metal' and 'plastic', prior to its disposal?

(a) In some States of the U.S.A. (b) In Southern England (c) In the Borough of London (d) In Central Tokyo.

266. Dr. P.C. Ray of Bengal was a famous scientist who helped in the revival of chemistry in India. Some of his books are mentioned here. Can you pick the false one?

(a) *The life and experience of a Bengali chemist* (b) *A history of Hindu Chemistry* (c) *The elements of chemistry* (d) *The place of science in literature*

267. Scientists are keen to know the age of rocks on earth or how old are the samples of rocks and dust brought back from the moon by astronauts. This can be found by determining, in the rock or dust, the proportion of radioactive:

(a) Uranium and stable lead (b) Potassium and stable calcium (c) Carbon and stable carbon (d) Radium and stable lead

268. When a dye is formed on the fibre or cloth by a chemical reaction at the time of dyeing, the process is known as:
(a) Vat dyeing (b) Direct dyeing (c) Synthesis (d) Absorption

269. Many experimental and practical uses of radioactive substances require separation of isotopes of their elements, that is, the lighter isotope is to be separated from the heavier one. This is carried out by the following methods. Can you pick the false one?
(a) Diffusion of gases (b) Electromagnetic separation (c) By irradiating with X-rays (d) By exchange reactions

270. Neutrinos are 'ghost particles' that have almost no weight and no electrical charge. They can pass through anything, even through the entire earth. One mile below the earth in South Dakota (U.S.A.) in a gold mine, attempts have been made to catch one or two ghost particles in:
(a) A magnetic field (b) A circular lead chamber (c) An electric tube (d) A tank of cleaning fluid

271. Metals are different from rocks, gases, salts, acids and bases. They have special

properties, such as metallic lustre, conduction of heat and electricity and imparting colours to flames. These special properties are caused by the presence of mobile electrons in a structure with a special chemical bond. Can you identify it?

(a) The covalent bond (b) The ionic bond (c) The hydrogen bond (d) The metal bond

272. '90-Octane petrol' is a rating that indicates that the petrol in the engine would not waste its energy in making a 'knocking sound', but would rather use its energy efficiently towards maintaining speed for travel. '90-Octane petrol' means that the petrol is as good as:

(a) A mixture of 90% iso-octane and 10% normal (straight chain) heptane (b) 90% normal heptane and 10% iso-octane (c) 90% octane (d) 90% petrol

273. Around 3,000 B.C., the Egyptians possessed 80% of the world's known gold. They knew how to make gold. The ore was crushed and heated in a charcoal fire till the melting point of gold was reached, which is:

(a) 252°C (b) 1063°C (c) 1574°C (d) 1985°C

274. Important uses of sodium carbonate are mentioned here. Can you pick the false one?

(a) In making tyres (b) In making soap (c) In baking of bread (d) In the making of paper

275. Emil Fischer, the eminent German chemist, was awarded the Nobel Prize for his pioneering work on sugar and purine synthesis in:
(a) 1920 (b) 1930 (c) 1911 (d) 1902

276. Iron nails rust fast when used for fixing plates or strips of aluminium on a building. Similarly, a water pipe made of iron corrodes faster when connected to a pipe of copper. This happens because of the:
(a) Higher rusting power of iron (b) Easier flow of electrons to iron (c) Greater wetting of iron (d) Chemical reduction of iron

277. Paraffin wax is a solid product obtained from petroleum. Some of its uses are mentioned here. Can you pick the false one?
(a) In the making of candles (b) As a coating on paper (c) In greases for axles of motor vehicles (d) As a stiffening agent in cosmetic creams

278. Which of the following is not a major air pollutant in the exhaust emitted from motor cars?
(a) Unburnt petrol (b) Carbon monoxide (c) Sulphur dioxide (d) Oxides of nitrogen

279. Susrutha, in ancient India, wrote a monumental work on chemistry, known as *Susrutha-Samhita*. Some observations on it are noted here. Can you pick the false one? (a) It mentioned metals and salts (b) It gave an account of the preparation and use of alkalis (c) It identified six metals (d) It treated mercury as a form of metal

280. Calcium carbonate can crystallize as calcite or as aragonite, having different crystal systems. These are called:
(a) Isomers (b) Polymers (c) Polymorphs (d) Mirror images

281. Electric bulbs were not there in olden times. Lighting (illumination) of houses at night by burning gases obtained from coal or wood was invented in England in the eighteenth century by:
(a) William Murdock (b) William Harvey (c) William Gilbert (d) John Bright

282. Nitrobenzene is used for making aniline, an important chemical used in:
(a) The crimping of wool (b) The dyeing industry (c) The making of glue (d) Fast-drying varnish

283. Metallurgy, the science of metals, known as 'Lohasastra' in India, was mentioned as far back as in:

(a) The eighteenth century works (b) The Vedas (c) The Jatakas, or Buddhist tales (d) The Rasratnakara by Nagarjuna

284. Alkaline earth metals are sparingly soluble in water and their carbonates evolve carbon dioxide on heating. Which of the following is not an alkaline earth metal?
(a) Beryllium (b) Magnesium (c) Calcium (d) Aluminium

285. Plastic articles like tubes, bottles, bowls, toy balls and fibre are made by various methods suited to each type of article. These methods are mentioned here. Can you pick the false one?
(a) Blow moulding for plastic bottles (b) Extrusion for plastic tubing (c) Rotational moulding for nylon filament yarn (d)Injection moulding for open type articles

286. Penicillin was a drug that saved many lives. Some facts about it are mentioned here. Can you pick the false one?
(a) Sir Alexander Fleming was awarded the Nobel Prize for its discovery (b) Flory was awarded the Nobel-Prize for its mass-production (c) The first patient was given his own urine containing pencillin because there was so little of it in the world, but he could not not be saved (d) When Flory applied pencillin directly on wounds, the doctors hailed him as a saviour

287. Pig iron can be converted into steel by removing a lot of carbon contained in it, in a:
(a) Blast furnace (b) Bessemer Converter (c) An electolytic chamber (d) A pyrite burner

288. Gases are sometimes finely scattered in a liquid, but they do not actually dissolve. These are known as colloidal solutions of gases in liquids. Some are mentioned here. Can you pick the false one?
(a) Froth (b) Whipped cream (c) Foams with very tiny bubbles (d) Mist

289. The earth is a round planet of solid matter surrounded by an envelope of air. If we go away from the sun towards the cold, outer parts of the solar system, we find that there are big planets which are mainly made of gases held together by gravity, with hardly any solid matter in them. Some are mentioned here. Can you pick the false one?
(a) Saturn (b) Jupiter (c) Mars (d) Uranus

290. Geiger-Muller counters and scintillation counters are instruments for measuring:
(a) The speed of chemical reactions (b) X-rays (c) Time (d) Radioactivity

291. 'I.U.P.A.C.' stands for
(a) International Units of Protein and Carbohydrates (b) International Union of Pure

and Applied Chemistry (c) Iodine Under-Packing (d) International Understanding on Physical Aspects of Chemistry

292. 'Thermal pollution' means dumping heat in an ecological system, like a lake or a pond. Thermal power plants have to throw some heat into a 'sink' because they:
(a) Follow the local sanitation laws (b) They have special anti-pollution laws (c) Get overheated (d) Follow the second natural law of thermodynamics

293. In some tropical islands of the Pacific, vehicles may move with their tyres a foot deep in the ground because the soil is non-sticky, like sand. This is due to the presence of oxides of aluminium and iron which:
(a) Cause dryness (b) Repel water (c) Prevent sticking of large particles of soil by coating them (d) Allow evaporation of water from the soil by making it porous

294. Flint, a fine-grained stone found in the earth was formed from the silica gel remains of very old siliceous plants and animals. Its uses are mentioned here. Can you pick the false one?
(a) Stone-age man used flint as a tool and weapon (b) Flint-locks were made in the seventeenth century (c) It was used as a substitute for chalk in the eighteenth century (d) In modern times, it is used for

grinding of cement and polishing of powders

295. Silt in water remains suspended. It is
removed by sedimentation and filtration.
For increasing its sedimentation aluminium
sulphates and calcium hydroxide (slaked
lime) are added. As a result sticky
aluminium hydroxide:
(a) Mixes with silt particles (b) Attracts the
particles of silt (c) Destroys silt particles
(d) Makes silt particles increase in size and
deposit at the bottom

296. Alkyd resins are made of glycerol. These
are used:
(a) As a substitute for white chalk (b) Instead of alkanes (c) For paints and coatings
(d) For making alcohol

297. Increase in standards of living has led to
a worldwide increase in the use and
consumption of materials. Therefore,
various possible sources of extraction are
being tried. Which of the following is a
new and unusual source of a material in
demand?
(a) Iodine from sea-weeds (b) Rare gases
from the air (c) Nickel metal from cultivation of plants (d) Iron from red-coloured
soil

298. Borax (sodium tetraborate) has many uses, some of which are mentioned here. Can you pick the false one?
(a) Making heat-resistant glass (b) In bleaching of paper pulp (c) For giving a glaze to linen, in laundering (d) As a flux in welding and soldering

299. We live in an age of nuclear weapons. When an atom of uranium-235 splits, it releases nuclear particles. These particles lead to great destruction, in the circumstances when:
(a) There is a controlled chain reaction (b) A volcano of heat (c) An uncontrolled chain reaction (d) Cosmic rays accompany them with shock waves and fire

300. In 1970, Har Gobind Khorana made a landmark in biochemistry for which he was awarded the Nobel Prize. He succeeded in:
(a) Making a protein (b) Making a vitamin (c) Discovered the structure of haemoglobin (d) Making a gene

Section 4

301. Some particles in nature are big, others are small. Others may be said to be neither big nor small, but on the borderline. For example, colloids may be more than a thousand times as big as an atom, but are more than thousand times smaller than an

ant. These colloids can be removed from a solution by a:
(a) Filter paper (b) Centrifuge (c) Thin piece of cloth (d) Parchment paper

302. Extremely dangerous and deadly cardiac glycosides are carried from the milkweed plant by the:
(a) Larvae of the monarch butterfly
(b) Bumble bee (c) Night cockroaches
(d) Green grasshopper

303. New types of opaque glasses have been introduced in the market for cooking utensils and kitchenware. The glass article does not break on heating. These special glasses are made by heating glass in the factory in such a way that in the glass:
(a) A thin layer of air bubbles is formed
(b) Many tiny crystals are formed (c) Some carbon is trapped (d) Some steel metal is fixed

304. Phosphorescence is the phenomenon observed when light passing through a substance gets absorbed and the substance continues to emit light and glow even in the dark when the light source is cut off. Which of the following is a phosphorescent substance?
(a) Diamond (b) Zinc sulphide (c) Gems
(d) Silver chloride

305. A polymer is formed when simple, chemical units:
(a) Break up (b) Combine to form long chains (c) Combine to form circles (d) Become round, complex shapes

306. Aluminium metal gets corroded or 'rusted' in places that are near to the sea, because the oxide film that protects it:
(a) Is removed by sea water (b) Reacts with water (c) Is attacked by salt from sea water (d) Reacts with sand particles

307. When oxygen gas is either absent or present in low quantity in the soil, in places like stagnant swamps, the soil is said to be in a:
(a) Chemically reducing (anaerobic) state
(b) Chemically oxidizing (aerobic) state
(c) Physical state of high viscosity
(d) Breathless, carbon dioxide environment

308. Turpentine is an oil used for dissolving paints. It is obtained from:
(a) The oak tree (b) The pine tree (c) Lemon (d) The birch tree

309. Catalysts, like platinum, hasten or slow down a chemical reaction, but remain unchanged at the end of the reaction. Wilhelm Ostwald conducted indepth research on how catalytic reactions take place and what determines the rate of a chemical reaction and chemical equilibrium. For this

work he was awarded the Nobel Prize for Chemistry in:
(a) 1900 (b) 1909 (c) 1931 (d) 1942

310. Chromium is used in making:
(a) Electrodes (b) Mosaic-floor grinders
(c) Stainless steel (d) Bronze

311. X-rays are produced when a stream of electrons in an X-ray tube:
(a) Hit the glass wall of the tube (b) Strike a metal target (c) Meet a thin ray of light
(d) Pass through a strong, magnetic field

312. Which of the following is not a mineral?
(a) Quartz (b) Mica (c) Feldspar (d) Peat

313. The atoms in a molecule do not remain stationary. They vibrate around their mean position, by stretching or bending out of the plane. We gain useful knowledge about these vibrations and the energy they carry by studying:
(a) Infrared spectra (b) Ultraviolet spectra
(c) X-ray spectra (d) Visible spectra

314. Unpainted pottery of a single colour is said to have been made as early as 7000 B.C. or even earlier. However, painting of pottery articles like bowls or flasks began around:
(a) 6500 B.C. (b) 3500 B.C. (c) 1500 B.C.
(d) A.D. 500

315. When fuel is added to the exhaust (burnt) gases in a jet engine, combustion takes place. Some facts are mentioned here about this combustion. Can you pick the false one?

(a) It gives additional thrust (b) It reduces fuel consumption (c) It increases the intake of oxygen from the air (d) It is known as 'after burning'

316. Many industries were discharging their effluent (waste) in the River Thames (Great Britain). This increased the temperature of the river and led to a decrease of oxygen in the river. A change like this, greatly, affects or destroys plants, fishes and other forms of aquatic life. It is known as:

(a) Oxygen decline (b) Water shield (c) Thermal pollution (d) The temperature effect

317. Charcoal obtained from wood has a large surface area because it has many pores. It is used in gas masks to adsorb some poisonous gases. It allows oxygen to pass through, but is able to adsorb the poisonous gas:

(a) Carbon dioxide (b) Hydrogen sulphide (c) Carbon monoxide (d) Chlorine

318. Casings of vacuum cleaners and sewing machines are made by casting magnesium metal in moulds. Magnesium is used in preference to other metals because it is:

(a) Tougher (b) Brighter (c) Lighter
(d) Smoother

319. Which of the following elements is not an essential constituent of a carbohydrate?
(a) Carbon (b) Oxygen (c) Hydrogen
(d) Nitrogen

320. Who was awarded the Nobel Prize for Chemistry in 1901 for discovering the laws of chemical dynamics and for studying the osmotic pressure of solutions?
(a) J. van't Hoff of Holland (b) Robinson of Britain (c) Pauling of U.S.A. (d) Svedberg of Sweden

321. Ships spend many years in the ocean, carrying passengers and freight. Their hulls get, severely, corroded by sea water and require replacement. To combat this problem, cathodic protection from rust formation is provided by:
(a) Plating with tin (b) Tying blocks of magnesium to the hull (c) Painting with white lead (d) Covering the bottom with a wire net of copper alloy

322. Various methods are adopted for protecting iron from rust. Which of the following statements is false?
(a)Zinc plating is more permanent than chrome plating (b) Ordinary tin plating is cheap but not reliable (c) Chrome plating

looks good (d) Zinc protects iron but does not protect itself.

323. When a mixture of sand, borax, alumina, soda and potassium carbonate are heated and melted, 'Borosilicate glass' is formed. This glass has the special property of being:
(a) Tough (b) Very transparent (c) Resistant to heat (d) Unbreakable

324 When on heating, a solid becomes vapour without forming any liquid, it is said to have sublimed. Which of the following sublimes on heating?
(a) Iron (b) Iodine (c) Salt (d) Calcium

325. The yellow colour of straw and wool can be removed by bleaching with a solution of:
(a) Sulphites (b) Nitrites (c) Iodine (d) Caustic soda

326. Termites are able to eat and destroy doors, windows, wooden furniture and other articles, because they have:
(a) Hard teeth made of calcium (b) Enzymes that digest cellulose (c) Claws that mesh wood into paper pulp (d) An acidic secretion that dissolves wood

327. Radon is a member of the noble gas family. Its radioactivity can be used for treatment of:

(a) Thyroid problems (b) Cancer
(c) Typhoid (d) Gallstones

328. Which of the following is a chemical change?
(a) Melting of sodium in a nuclear reactor
(b) Sublimation of iodine (c) Explosion of dynamite (d) Condensation of steam

329. Which solvent is used for dry-cleaning of clothes?
(a) Acetone (b) Alcohol (c) Carbon tetrachloride (d) Freon

330. Which of the following artificial sweeteners was banned in 1969 in the U.S., when it was suspected that it may be carcinogenic (cancer causing)?
(a) Saccharin, which is 300 times sweeter than sugar (b) Cyclamates, which are 30 times sweeter than sugar (c) Aspartame, which is 180 times sweeter than sugar (d) Glycine, a sweet amino acid

331. Which of the following methods of waste disposal would be expected to immediately cause great pollution?
(a) Burning waste in an incinerator
(b) Sanitary landfills (c) Stream discharge
(d) Radioactive waste packing

332. Some substances that show fluorescence are mentioned here. Can you pick the false one?

(a) Anthracene shows a violet fluorescence
(b) Naphthacene shows green fluorescence
(c) Fluorescein (d) Radium

333. Modern oil-based paints contain oils that can dry to form strong, adhesive films by cross-linking of fatty acid chains. Some of these 'drying oils' are mentioned here. Can you pick the false one?
(a) Soyabean (b) Turpentine oil (c) Linseed oil (d) Castor oil

334. Calcium is abundantly distributed in nature in combination with other elements. Some minerals which contain calcium are mentioned here. Can you pick the false one?
(a) Marble and limestone (b) Chalk and calcite (c) Ilmenite and Carnotite (d) Iceland spar and Gypsum

335. The salt that we eat is 'common salt'. Its natural form is present in sea water. In chemical language, the word 'salt' has a wider meaning. Can you tell which of the following salts is the one that we add to our food for a salty taste and which is an essential nutrient for millions of plants, animals and living organisms?
(a) Ferric sulphate (b) Potassium iodide (c) Copper nitrate (d) Sodium chloride

336. The ashes of plants contain alkali metals, 90% of which is:

(a) Sodium (b) Potassium (c) Lithium
(d) Rubidium

337. At night when the lights of a scooter or a
car fall on a road-sign or on a vehicle
moving ahead, the painted letters or numbers shine with a glow. Which of the
following is a luminous paint?
(a) Zinc sulphide (b) Barium sulphide
(c) Nickel-chrome alloy (d) Silver-plated
metal

338. This wonderful acid has many uses. It is
used for making explosives, pigments,
dyes, hydrochloric acid, in sulphonation of
oils to make detergents and in lead ac-
cumulators. Can you identify it?
(a) Nitric acid (b) Caustic soda (c) Sulphuric acid (d) Zinc chloride

339. Research and Development units are being
set up in many chemical industries. Which
of the following countries is recognized
more for basic research in comparison to
its achievements and contributions in Technology and Engineering?
(a) Japan (b) Great Britain (c) Sweden
(d) Korea

340. The burning of wood and coal for cooking
at home and in industries and the burning
of diesel and petrol, releases a lot of carbon
dioxide in the air. To absorb it one would
need to grow a forest bigger than Australia

every year. Nature has arranged that half of this carbon dioxide gets absorbed by:
(a) Mountain ranges (b) Ocean waters (c) Snow and hail (d) Glaciers

341. Some parts of the world that are known to be richly endowed with petroleum deposits, based on major oil discoveries mentioned here. Can you pick the false one?
(a) The Middle East (b) U.S.S.R. (c) Australia (d) The North Sea.

342. Stains of ink or rust from iron on clothes, tables and sheets can be best removed by:
(a) Hydrogen peroxide (b) Alcohol (c) Oxalic acid (d) Petrol

343. When steam is blown over white-hot coke, we get:
(a) Water gas (b) Ammonia (c) Carbon dioxide (d) Inert gas

344. 'Bouncing putty' is a toy-like substance that is in a state between a liquid and a solid. If it is thrown on the wall, it bounces back like a ball. But, if it is placed on the table, it collapses into a thick liquid. It is made of:
(a) Polythene (b) Tyre rubber (c) Silicone rubber (d) Fibreglass treated with wax

345. Many metals, like, chromium, molybdenum, cobalt and nickel become inert

(chemically unreactive) on adding concentrated:
(a) Caustic soda (b) Nitric acid (c) Barium sulphate (d) A solution of bromine in water

346. Ordnance factories that make arms and ammunition use gun metal, which is made of bronze along with some lead and zinc that are added to:
(a) Give strength (b) Machine the metal easily (c) Add finish (d) Add dark colour

347. Acetic acid is used in making many things, some of which are mentioned here. Can you pick the false one?
(a) Aspirin for curing headaches (b) Artificial silk (c) Perfume sprays (d) Mineral water

348. If you watch a burning candle carefully, you will find different colours in the flame. Which is the hottest part of the candle flame?
(a) The outermost portion that is blue (b) The middle, yellow part (c) The middle orange part (d) The innermost black zone

349. Foam rubber is used in making mattresses for a soft bed, pillow or sofa cushions. The rubber foam is produced by the passage of oxygen through rubber-forming material, like the baking of bread from a paste of wheat and water (the dough). This oxygen for making foam is released from:

(a) Carbon dioxide (b) Baking soda
(c) Nitric oxide (d) Hydrogen peroxide

350. Sulphur is used in many things. Can you pick the false one?
(a) In the manufacture of sulphuric acid
(b) Vulcanization of rubber (c) In the black colour of shoe polish (d) Protection of grape wines

351. Submarines move under water. They have engines that run on:
(a) Petrol and oxygen (b) Diesel (c) Batteries (d) Steam

352. Archaelogists and museum curators find it difficult to preserve old statues and relics, which get faded or withered with the passage of time by the action of air, dust and moisture. To protect these old, historical art treasures, they are covered with a tight, transparent film of:
(a) Nylon (b) Viscose (c) Silicone
(d) Polythene

353. When metal foundry products are cleaned by shot blasting, heat is generated by friction. Nitrogen is used for:
(a) Reducing friction (b) Cooling the blast chamber (c) Providing an inert atmosphere
(d) Displacing hot air

354. The lightest element in the world is:

(a) Hydrogen (b) helium (c) Oxygen
(d) Chlorine

355. Tartaric acid is a colourless, crystalline acid
found in fruit juices, like that of grapes.
Some of its uses are mentioned here. Can
you pick the false one?
(a) In dyeing of cloth (b) In cosmetics
(c) In photography (d) In medicines

356. Gold cannot be dissolved by any acid.
However, it can be dissolved by aqua regia
(kingly water) which is a mixture of:
(a) Water and sulphur (b) Nitric and
hydrochloric acids (c) Mineral water and
Iodine (d) Alcohol and alum

357. Scientists are trying to get energy from
oceans as they contain heavy water. This
energy will come from a hot, nuclear
reaction that will melt the toughest container. Therefore, the reaction has been
carried out in a bottle made of:
(a) Magnetic forces (b) Sound waves
(c) Vacuum (d) X-ray beams

358. Copper is a metal in great demand. Its ores
contain very little copper. It is therefore
concentrated by removing sand, rock and
clay before melting it in the furnace. The
part of the ore that is richly endowed with
copper sulphide is obtained as a froth by
agitating with:

(a) Lemon juice (b) Pine oil (c) Pineapple juice (d) Eucalyptus oil

359. The cobalt hexammine cation has an atom of cobalt in the centre, surrounded by six molecules of ammonia that are attatched to it. The shape of this ion is:
(a) Linear (b) Square (c) Tetrahedral (d) Octahedral

360. The metal ions (charged particles) that are required for contraction of muscles in human beings and animals are ions of:
(a) Potassium (b) Sodium (c) Calcium (d) Iron

361. The Nobel Prize in Chemistry is awarded for a noteworthy discovery in this field with a gold medal and an honorarium of over a hundred thousand dollars at a grand ceremony at Stockholm every year in December. In 1924 no award was given. Some other years are mentioned below, when no award was given. Can you pick the false one?
(a) 1916 (b) 1917 (c) 1918 (d) 1919

362. 'Guttapercha' is a tough, crystalline, thermoplastic. It is:
(a) A type of nylon sheet (b) A synthetic rubber (c) An isomer of natural rubber (d) The thread of terylene

363. Bleaching powder has several uses, some of which are mentioned here. Can you pick the false one?
(a) For sterilizing water (b) For bleaching paper pulp (c) For decolourising sugar (d) For making chloroform

364. Monel metal is a metallic alloy of copper and nickel with 5% iron. It is used in making:
(a) Almirahs (b) Strong boxes (c) Locks (d) Motor parts

365. If you splash a glass of water in the ocean and Nature mixes it well with all the water in the world, then every glass of water in the world will contain a very, very small part of the water thrown by you, which will be:
(a) One molecule thrown from your glass
(b) Two molecules from your glass
(c) Twenty molecules from your glass
(d) Two hundred molecules from your glass

366. Detergents have the advantage over soaps that they:
(a)Wash clothes whiter (b) Absorb the hardness of water (c) Are less affected by hard water (d) Are less soapy

367. Gases like helium, neon and xenon have a special atomic structure that makes them chemically quite inert. They are also rare

in their natural occurrence on earth. The presence of these rare gases was discovered by Sir William Ramsay of Great Britain, for which he was awarded the Nobel Prize in:

(a) 1904 (b) 1916 (c) 1928 (d) 1940

368. Irritation from the bite of some insects, and the stinging sensation of nettles is caused by:

(a) Aniline (b) Formic acid (c) Sulphuric acid (d) Caustic soda

369. A ship travelling in the open ocean cannot take energy from the ocean and convert it into useful work because the temperature of the:

(a) Ship can never be higher than that of the ocean (b) Ocean can never be higher than that of the ship (c) Ocean and of the ship are never equal (d) Ocean is more than 25°C.

370. Nuclear reactors that make fissionable materials like Plutonium-239, are known as:

(a) Breeder reactors (b) Fissile reactors (c) Plutonium converters (d) Nuclear stations

371. Nine planets revolve round the sun. The outer, distant planets are Jupiter, Saturn, Neptune Uranus and Pluto. In comparison to these, the 'inner planets', Mercury,

Venus, Earth and Mars that are nearer to the centre of the sun contain relatively:
(a) Heavier elements of matter (b) Lighter elements (c) New elements of matter (d) Larger quantities of gas

372. Acetaldeleyde can be used for making synthetic:
(a) Rubbers (b) Perfumes (c) Protein (d) Sugar

373. Oil is found in great quantities in some places under huge pressure. Which of the following is incorrect?
(a) The gushing oil can throw off a crane like a toy (b) The oil can collect in a size big enough to float a navy (c) The gushing oil can reach a mile up in the sky (d) Precaution is necessary against fire hazard

374. Natural rubber is obtained as 'latex', which is a milky, white fluid from rubber trees. Latex is a:
(a) Solution of rubber in water (b) Colloidal dispersion of rubber in water (c) Mixture of rubber and gum (d) Paste of rubber, clay and water

375. With the advancement of ocean technology, sea bed treaties are being concluded by nations, demanding exclusive economic rights because of the realization that vast deposits of mineral resources lie on the sea

bed. A rich source of metals from the sea bed are:

(a) Deep sea plants (b) Polymetallic nodules (c)Sea mountains (d) Sea weeds

376. Every year more than 10,000 tonnes of mercury is mined all over the world. Mercury is toxic to human and animal life. Pollution control of mercury is achieved by adding sodium sulphide which precipitates mercury sulphide in a mud. When the mud is stirred with a solution of chlorine and sodium hydroxide:

(a) Lead is removed (b) Mercury is destroyed (c) It becomes non-toxic (d) Mercury is recovered

377. Acidity of the soil is of great importance for agriculture. Which of the following plants tolerate a strongly acidic soil and grow well in it?

(a) Tea (b) Pineapples (c) Beans (d) Blueberries

378. Teflon, a polymer of tetrafluoroethylene, is an excellent plastic material for films and coatings. Some of its very useful qualities are mentiored here. Can you pick the false one?

(a) It is one of the most chemically-resistant plastics in the world (b) It can withstand high temperatures (c) It is unaltered by radiation (d) It is an ideal insulator for high-frequency fittings

93

379. The retina is a delicate spot that receives images through the eye lens and makes us see the world. If it gets detatched, it is very difficult to join it back. Therefore, eye surgeons use:
(a) Micro-knives for surgery (b) Sound waves for joining (c) Laser-beams for welding the retina (d) Ultraviolet rays for surgery

380. Zinc chromate and lead chromate are used as:
(a) Mordants (b) Lacquers (c) Lakes (d) Pigments

381. Sensitized silver bromide paper is used in photographic reels of cameras. When light falls on it, it forms dark, minute particles of:
(a) Bromine (b) Silver (c) Silver bromide (d) Paper

382. Selenium has the unusual property of being a bad conductor in light but a poor conductor in the dark. It was, therefore, used in making:
(a) Solar hats (b) Photo-electric cells (c) Shaded glass (d) Chromatic lenses

383. Polonium is a radioactive element. Its discoverer named it after:
(a) The game of polo that he liked (b) Her country Poland (c) Her parrot, Polly (d) Her friend's polite nature

384. A proton is a small, positive particle of the tiny atom. It moves much faster in ice than in water, as if to say, it was:
(a) Jumping through a tunnel in the ice (b) Rotating at a great speed in ice (c) Cutting ice (d) Floating at random

385. Lead, a metal, is formed when its sulphide ore is heated in air to form the oxide and then reduced in a small blast furnace with:
(a) Magnesium (b) Iron (c) Carbon (d) Silicon

386. We know that meteorites fall from outer space making huge craters on the earth and on the moon. They are of different types, depending on what they are made of and their texture. Which of the following is not a type of meteorite?
(a) Iron meteorites (b) Stony meteorites (c) Fireclay meteorites (d) Glassy meteorites

387. Clouds, mist, fog and aerosols (such as perfumes and sprays) are colloidal solutions of a:
(a) Solid in a gas (b) Gas in a solid (c) Liquid in a gas (d) Gas in a liquid

388. Beautiful colours of fireworks are produced by adding salts of various metals into the burning mixture. The firework colours of different metals are mentioned here. Can you pick the false one?

(a) Copper gives a green light (b) Sodium gives a yellow light (c) Calcium gives a brick-red light (d) Strontium gives a blue light

389. A chelating agent is a chemical that catches a metal ion (charged particle) in its 'claw'. Pencillin can remove excesses of a metal by chelation in the ailment known as Wilson's disease. The metal chelated by penicillin is:
(a) Iron (b) Copper (c) Nickel (d) Molybdenum

390. Which of the following is not essential for rust to form?
(a) Oxygen (b) Iron (c) Water (d) Carbon dioxide

391. When nitrogen from the air is utilized by living organisms and fixed in chemical compounds, the soil becomes richer in nitrogen and more fertile. This fixation of nitrogen can be done by blue-green algae and also by bacteria of the genus Rhizobium when they grow on the roots of the plants mentioned here. Can you pick the false one?
(a) Peas (b) Tomatoes (c) Beans (d) Alfalfa

392. Teflon (tetrafluoroethylene) is a black material used in non-stick pans for frying chips and vegetables. The oil or butter does

not stick at all. In the process of manufacture, one of the technical problems is:
(a) To make teflon (b) To make teflon that is non-sticky (c) To make teflon stick to the metal of the pan (d) To cut a round sheet of teflon that exactly fits

393. Using special techniques of high temperature and pressure with a suitable catalyst like tantalum, graphite can be converted into:
(a) Lead (b) Charcoal (c) Synthetic coal (d) Synthetic diamonds

394. Which of the following gases, in pure form, has a slightly blue colour?
(a) Carbon dioxide (b) Oxygen (c) Ozone (d) Hydrogen

395. Creams for applying on the hair have a nozzle spray fitted on the top of the container. You can spray on your hair for a convenient distribution of cream. The gas that is used to disperse and spray hair creams is:
(a) Fluoroform (b) Chloroform (c) Methane (d) Ammonia

396. Human beings cannot digest grass or hay. Horses, cattle and sheep can eat and digest grass or hay because:
(a) They have strong teeth (b) They have a special enzyme in their stomach (c) Their

blood is different (d) Grass is delicious for their tongues

397. During the First World War, a poison gas called Lewisite was used, which contained arsenic. A chelating agent was developed that was non-poisonous and competed against the chemical poison by 'catching' the heavy metals in the body which the poison was trying to trap. This defensive chemical was known as:
(a) A sulpha drug (b) British anti-Lewisite (c) Carbolic acid (d) A catalytic agent

398. The scientists, Perutz and Kendrew worked for several years studying the structures of big complicated biological molecules, taking X-ray pictures of their crystals. They were awarded the Nobel Prize for discovering the structure of globular (round) proteins that dissolve in water such as:
(a) Keratin of hair (b) Haemoglobin of blood (c) Collagen (d) Myosin of muscles

399. When ammonium nitrate is mixed with aluminium powder, we get 'ammonal', which is:
(a) A paint (b) A solvent (c) An explosive (d) A dye

400. Michaelangelo, the renowned sculptor, found a pure, white variety of marble from which he thought of making a huge statue as a landmark for passing ships. This marble belonged to a place in Italy called:

(a) Pisa and contained upto 98% pure copper oxide (b) Martigny and contained upto 50% clay (c) Alessandria and contained pure chrome (d) Carrara and contained upto 98% calcium carbonate

Section 5

401. When a substance reacts with water and breaks into acids and bases the process is called:
(a) Hydrolysis (b) Solvolysis (c) Dialysis (d) Dissolution

402. Everyone has heard of arsenic poisoning. Even 0.1 gram of arsenic oxide can be fatal. If consumed by mistake, the antidote is freshly precipitated:
(a) Sodium chloride (b) Ferrous nitrate (c) Ferric hydroxide (d) Ferric sulphate

403. Which of the following elements has a relatively stable nucleus (centre of the atom)?
(a) Uranium (b) Hydrogen (c) Iron (d) Radium

404. Methyl bromide is made by the action of bromine gas on methane. Some of its uses are mentioned here. Can you pick the false one ?
(a) It is an insecticide (b) It disinfects nursery stock of plants before transplanting (c) It disinfects young fruit trees (d) It is used for dyeing cloth

405. When ice is heated it has a natural preference to use the heat to melt and become water at the same temperature, namely 0°C. It appears to have a choice to remain as ice and to use the heat to increase its temperature, but it does not do so. The reason for the preference to melt is that:
(a) Water has a more ordered structure than ice (b) Natural processes prefer to move towards more ordered arrangements (c) There is a decline in entropy (a scientific indicator of disorder in a system) (d) There is more disorder in the structure of water than in ice

406. 'Buna-N rubber' is a copolymer of butadiene and acrylonitrile. In comparision to natural rubber it:
(a) Is a poor substitute for natural rubber
(b) Has better resistance to wear and tear
(c) Is delicate and soft (d) Does not last for a long time

407. DNA is the material in the body that determines the height, colour of eyes, face and hair of children and future generations. DNA is a biochemical that consists of two strands, each having the shape of a:
(a) Bow tie (b) Rose petal (c) Circular staircase (d) Wave

408. Phosphorous can exist in four different allotropic forms mentioned here. Can you pick the false one?
(a) White phosphorous (b) Red phorphorous (c) Scarlet phosphorous and black phosphorous (d) Green phosphorous and blue phosphorous

409. Currency notes can be marked with an invisible ink. Thieves can be trapped because this ink:
(a) Turns blue on adding acid (b) Turns red on adding alkali (c) Shows up in ultraviolet light (d) Is attracted by a magnet

410. For walls of buildings a white wash can be made that is resistant to weather. This white wash has a water proof film that is made by adding hydrated lime to milk protein (say, from skimmed milk) and:
(a) Soda (b) Formaldehyde (c) Vinegar (d) Sugar

411. In some places whisky is stored in earthenware pots that have not been properly glazed. This may cause poisoning by:
(a) Lead (b) Copper (c) Nickel (d) Tin

412. Shells and corals of the sea contain calcium in the form of:
(a) Aragonite (b) Calcite (c) Marble (d) Iceland spar

413. Vinylite resins are copolymers of vinyl acetate and vinyl chloride. They are resis-

tant to wear and tear and to chemicals. One of their well-known uses is in:
(a) Tyres (b) Ropes (c) Floor coverings (d) Electrical insulators

414. Some scientists believe that a chemical widely used as a preservative and a colouring agent in foods gets converted to an acid in the stomach, affects the genes and causes cancer in human beings. Can you identify the substance?
(a) Vinegar (b) Sodium nitrite (c) Ferric chloride (d) Sulphur dioxide

415. One way of preventing pollution of the air is by passing exhaust gases through a filter. Glass fibre or silicone-treated bags of textile material are used for filtering:
(a) Cold gases (b) High pressure gases (c) Hot gases (d) Reactive gases

416. An 'Ion' is a three-letter word. It means:
(a) A charged particle (b) An alloy of iron (c) A mixture of Iodine, Oxygen and Nitrogen (d) A form of light

417. White paints made of white lead get blackened in cities after sometime because of chemical reaction with one of the following pollutants present in the air. Can you identify it?
(a) Carbon dioxide (b) Sulphur dioxide (c) Carbon monoxide (d) Industrial soot (carbon)

418. Spectroscopic studies of distant light coming from planets in our solar system show that methane, an organic gas, which is associated with living matter on Earth, is present on some planets. Can you pick the false one?
(a) Mars (b) Jupiter (c) Mercury (d) Saturn

419. Everyday many new chemicals are being made. However, some chemicals are so basic that they are used in almost every industry. Which of the following is the most important industrial chemical?
(a) Nitric acid (b) Sulphuric acid (c) Alcohol (d) Acetone

420. Which of the following is a steel that is resistant to acids?
(a) Stainless steel (b) Molybdenum steel (c) Nickel alloy steel (d) Cobalt alloy steel

421. Fake art objects can be detected by scientific methods. The composition of bronze metal in olden times was different from that of today. If anyone claims that a fake statue is very old, a piece of bronze taken from it can be tested by:
(a) Dissolving it in acid (b) Rubbing off the fake dust (c) A magnet (d) Recording its spectrum

422. Cancer is a desease where body cells grow unchecked. A protein found in the body interferes with the growth of cancer cells.

It is used for the treatment of cancer. Can you identify it?
(a) Keratin (b) Casein (c) Haemoglobin (c) Interferon

423. When matter meets anti-matter, they destroy each other and vanish in a flash of energy and light. This has been proven by scientists to be a true fact in respect of some of the tiny particles of matter mentioned here. Can you pick the false one (that has not been discovered at all)?
(a) The anti-matter of the electron (discovered in 1931) (b) An anti-proton (discovered in 1955) (c) An anti-neutron (discovered in 1956) (d) An anti-atom (discovered in 1970)

424. Molecules have various shapes. Some moleules that have a linear shape are mentioned here. Can you pick the false one?
(a) Carbon dioxide (b) Acetylene (c) Mercurous chloride (d) Methane

425. It is extremely bad to kill animals for ivory. As far back as 1·897, a good substitute was found for ivory by making moulds of pigments with:
(a) Fat from butter (b) Casein from skimmed milk (c) Groundnut oil (d) Chalk and alcohol

426. Which of the following explode on heating?

(a) Chlorides (b) Sulphates (c) Azides
(d) Phosphides

427. In the London Museum, there is a colloidal solution of gold that was made by the well-known scientist, Michael Faraday in 1857. The gold:
(a) Has, with the passage of time, precipitated (settled at the bottom) (b) Has partially evaporated (c) Has turned red over the years (d) Has remained unchanged

428. Mercury is a silvery-white, shining liquid It has the power to dissolve many metals. A mixture of a metal dissolved in mercury is popularly known as:
(a) A mercury salt (b) An alloy (c) An amalgam (d) A solution

429. Iron is an essential nutrient for plants, which absorb it from the soil. Iron deficiency is often found in wet, clayey soils that have a high content of:
(a) Phosphate (b) Chloride (c) Carbonate (d) Sulphate

430. A chemical contained in tea is also contained in the bark of a tree. It is used for making ink-removers. Can you identify it?
(a) Tannic acid (b) Oxalic acid (c) Caffeine (d) Cellulose

431. Spacecraft like the satellites that circle the earth and are used in television transmis-

sion, have electric batteries that supply power for various purposes. These batteries contain ion-exchange resins instead of a liquid electrolyte solution because:
(a) A high electric voltage is required (b) Of lack of oxygen (c) Of extreme cold conditions (d) Of zero gravity

432. Eclogite is the world's most dense rock of siliceous matter. It is used for roads, abrasives and monuments. It sometimes contains:
(a) Lead (b) Chromium (c) Diamonds (d) Uranium

433. Chlorophyll, the green colouring matter in plants helps the process of photosynthesis by:
(a) Reacting with carbon dioxide (b) Converting soil into carbohydrates (c) Acting as a catalyst (d) Fixing soil nitrogen

434. A solid can be irreversibly deformed. The stamping of sheets of steel into 'fins' of motor cars is a case of:
(a) Elastic deformation (b) Plastic deformation (c) Vacuum deformation (d) Flexible shaping

435. There is indirect evidence that the core (centre) of the earth is a liquid with a density similar to liquid iron at high pressure. This evidence comes from a

study of the natural phenomena mentioned here. Can you pick the false one?
(a) Earthquakes (b) Ice-caps at the poles (c) Tidal waves in the oceans (d) Magnetism

436. A buffer country is a neutral state that lies between two opposing camps. In chemistry, a buffer helps in maintaining the:
(a) Acidity or alkalinity of a solution (b) Alkalinity of solids (c) Distance between two gases (d) The difference between gases and solids

437. Which of the following is a flavouring agent known as 'Oil of Wintergreen'?
(a) Olive oil (b) Methyl salicylate (c) Vinegar (d) Tartaric acid

438. Carbon disulphide is a very good solvent. Which of the following cannot be dissolved by it ?
(a) Rubber (b) Oils and fats (c) Sulphur, bromine and iodine (d) Sugar and proteins

439. A very pure form of carbon monoxide can be obtained from:
(a) Formic acid (b) Sodium oxalate (c) Sodium hexacyanoferrate (d) Nickel tetracarbonyl

440. Gold is dearly possessed by millions of people as jewellery, coins and articles. If all the gold in the world were to be stored in rooms ten feet long, ten feet wide and

ten feet high, how many rooms would it occupy?
(a) 2 (b) 12 (c) 160 (d) 800

441. The brilliance of diamonds is due to the internal reflection of light. The light is slowed down and bent away from its original path because it strikes:
(a) Loosely-held mobile electrons (b) The nucleus (centre) of carbon atoms (c) Tightly-bound electrons (d) Layers of carbon atoms

442. Which of the following is not a synthetic rubber?
(a) Buna-S rubber (b) Buna-N rubber (c) Neoprene (d) Polyethylene

443. German silver is used for making beautiful cutlery, jewellery or tea sets. It is made of 60% copper along with:
(a) Nickel and zinc (b) Cobalt and iron (c) Chromium and lead (d) Silver and lithium

444. Calamine is an important ore of zinc, in the form of carbonate. It occurs in cavities and veins of limestone. Some of its colour forms are mentioned here. Can you pick the false one?
(a) White (b) Red (c) Green (d) Brown

445. Hydrazine is a constitutent of drugs that are used for the treatment of:

(a) Typhoid (b) Tuberculosis (c) Cholera (d) Malaria

446. Different dyes are used for dyeing different materials. Which of the following statements is false?
(a) Terylene is mainly dyed with disperse dyes (b) Cotton can be directly dyed with malachite green (c) Nylon can be dyed with acid dyes (d) Polyacrylonitrile can be dyed with basic dyes

447. Boron nitride has a giant, cross-linked, three-dimensional structure which gives rise to the properties mentioned here. Can you pick the false one?
(a) It is chemically unreactive (b) Its structure is like that of diamond and is, therefore, hard (c) It can be melted only under pressure at a very high temperature of 3,000°C (d) It has magnetic properties

448. Objects falling from outer space contain evidence that there may be life outside this earth. A meteorite from space that fell on earth was found to contain 6 percent organic matter and there were chains of carbon upto 29 atoms long, distributed in their molecular weight in the same fashion as the carbon atoms in butter. This surprising event happened in:
(a) 1965 at Belgaum (India) (b) 1864 at Orgueil (France) (c) 1730 at Sheffield

(England) (d) 1520 at Wake Islands (Pacific Ocean)

449. Ductility is the property of a substance that allows it to be easily stretched into a wire. A small piece of silver weighing just one gram, can be drawn into a wire:
(a) One inch long (b) Ten inches long (c) Ten feet long (d) Two miles long

450. Emulsions of polyvinyl acetate are used in:
(a) Crayons (b) Firecrackers (c) Polishes (d) Latex paints

451. The metal palladium can absorb in the space between its atoms, 900 times its volume of hydrogen, which makes palladium a very useful industrial catalyst. This is known as:
(a) Absorption (b) Chemisorption (c) Addition (d) Deposition

452. Hydrocyanic acid is very:
(a) light (b) bright (c) explosive (d) poisonous

453. Known as the 'chemist of the twentieth century', he explained the chemical behaviour of matter in terms of the chemical bond between two atoms, which serves even today as a useful school of thought for explaining the chemical structure and behaviour of matter. He won the Nobel Prize for this in 1954. Can you identify him?

(a) Enrico Fermi (b) Niels Bohr (c) Linus Pauling (d) Paul H. Nernst

454. Topaz, opal, agate and onyx are precious and beautiful stones found in nature. All these are different forms of:
(a) Carbon (b) Soda (c) Silica (d) Lime

455. Magnetic ceramics or ferrites contain compounds of iron. These have been used:
(a) For building water-desalinators on ships
(b) As memory elements in computers
(c) In panels for solar cells (d) For making transformers

456. L.S.D. causes hallucinations. The full chemical name of this drug is:
(a) Lithium sulphide (b) Lysergic acid diethylamide (c) Dextro-lysine (d) Lanthanum sulphide

457. If you stretch an ordinary rubber-band on your mouth, it feels warm because it loses heat. On contracting, the rubber-band feels cool because it takes up heat from the mouth. The contraction of the rubber-band is a spontaneous, natural process because it is acompanied by:
(a) An increase in heat in the rubber-band
(b) A decrease in the free-energy in the rubber-band (c) An increase in the kinetic energy (d) An elastic force

458. Chocolates and fatty foods containing butter or oil sometimes leave stains on clothes that are difficult to remove. They can be removed by:

(a) Water (b) Tetrachloroethylene (c) A solution of salt in water (d) Alcohol

459. Some soaps do not fall to the bottom of the bath tub if they, accidentally, slip from the hand, while taking a bath. They are known as floating soaps. They float on water because they are made:

(a) From light sandalwood (b) From sponge rubber dipped in soap (c) By beating air into the soap (d) By adding pieces of cork

460. It is sometimes necessary to remove colouring matter contained as an impurity in glass. Glass is decolourised by:

(a) Bleaching powder (b) Manganese dioxide (c) Wood charcoal (d) Hydrogen

461. Titanium oxide is added in interior paints for walls of rooms, halls and galleries to give:

(a) A redder 'red' (b) A greener 'green'
(c) A whiter 'white' (d) Silver-white

462. Furfural, an organic chemical obtained by distilling oat husks or cotton seed hulls has many uses, some of which are mentioned here. Can you pick the false one?

(a) In refining of petroleum (b) For making plastics (c) As a solvent in the manufacture of rubber (d) For making fireworks

463. Aspirin, a drug for curing headaches and pains, is:
(a) Anthraquinone (b) Acetylsalicylic acid (c) Pyridine (d) Benzaldehyde

464. Which organic chemical bond between two carbon atoms can be easily disrupted?
(a) A single bond (b) A double bond (c) A triple bond (d) An aromatic ring

465. A photocell converts light into electric signals. It is used in burglar alarms and for tapping light energy from the sun. Which metal is widely used in photocells?
(a) Sodium (b) Tungsten (c) Caesium (d) Silver-plated steel

466. Old tin plates can be reused by removing the coating of tin on the metal. This saves a lot of money on buying new metal. The tin is removed with the help of:
(a) Oxygen (b) Metal brushes (c) Solvents (d) Chlorine

467. Hydrogen, nitrogen and oxygen are gases at ordinary room temperature. They can be liquefied by cooling. The liquid form of these gases is held together by a weak attraction among the molecules, knows as:

(a) Van der Waals' attraction (b) Gravitational attraction (c) Nuclear attraction (d) Magnetic attraction

468. The most common element in the earth's crust is oxygen. The second most common element is:
(a) Iron (b) Silicon (c) Copper (d) Aluminium

469. Food is packed in tins. As long as the tin is not punctured, it does not rust. As soon as it is punctured, the iron starts rusting fast because:
(a) Tin does not protect iron (b) Tin starts reacting with iron (c) Oxygen begins to react with tin (d) Iron starts protecting tin from rust

470. In some parts of the Hawaii islands in the Pacific, the soil is very red in colour. The red colour is due to:
(a) Cobalt (b) The oxidized form of iron (c) Potash (d) Iron in ferrous (reduced) form

471. A dye-intermediate is thought to be the cause of cancer of the bladder in workers working in a dye-making factory. Can you identify the dye?
(a) Beta-naphthylamine (b) Aniline (c) Indigo (d) A Vat dye

472. Dials of watches used to be painted with radium that made them glow at night. Radium, however, was harmful, being a radioactive element. Nowadays, other luminous paints are used. Which of the following is a luminous paint used for making hands of watches that glow?
(a) Zinc sulphide (b) Barium platinocyanide (c) Phosphorous (d) Red lead

473. When vegetable oils are reacted with hydrogen gas, using nickel metal as a catalyst, we get:
(a) Saturated fat (Artificial ghee, a form of butter) (b) Washing soaps (c) Carbon dioxide and water (d) Oil or lacquers and paints

474. A nuclear reactor can be cooled by transferring heat generated from the reactor to a turbine steam boiler. Which of the following materials is used in transferring this heat?
(a) Iron vapour (b) Compressed hydrogen (c) Radioactive carbon (d) Molten sodium

475. According to the Big Bang theory, the Universe was a small, compact ball that exploded with a loud noise and started expanding:
(a) A million years ago (b) A billion years ago (c) Four billion years ago (d) Five trillion years ago

476. Friedrich Mohs, the Viennese mineralogist, developed a scale of measuring hardness of substances. Some parts of the scale are mentioned here. Can you pick the false one?
(a) Talc is scratched by a finger nail
(b) Calcite is scratched by a copper coin
(c) Quartz scratches topaz (d) Diamond cannot be scratched

477. An atom is very small. There are billions of atoms on the tip of a pointed needle. In 1970, Dr. Creme announced that he had photographed an atom. Photographing the atom was, earlier, a dream for scientists. Dr. Creme achieved this by using
(a) A telescope (b) A scanning electron microscope (c) An X-ray picture tube (d) A beam of fast-moving hydrogen ions

478. Tin is a silvery-white, soft metal that can exist in three allotropic forms, which are mentioned here. Can you pick the false one?
(a) Grey tin (b) Brown tin (c) White tin
(d) Rhombic tin

479. There are various arsenic drugs (containing arsenic compounds), such as Sylvarsan, Atoxyl and Tryparsamine. Their main use is in treatment of:
(a) Jaundice (b) Typhoid (c) Syphilis
(d) Cholera

480. Lighter gases can diffuse faster than heavier ones. This is used for separating on a large scale:
(a) Iron and copper (b) The isotopes of uranium used in nuclear fission (c) Chlorine and oxygen (d) Salt from sea water

481. Crystals have 'vacant sites' or 'defects' in them. When light strikes a photographic silver bromide paper, silver atoms move in through these defects to:
(a) Form negative images (b) Form tiny clumps of silver atoms (c) Develop the film (d) Form a colour image

482. Optical whiteners are used for making clothes whiter. They are marketed under various brand names. They give a more white appearance to white shirts, sheets and other clothing by:
(a) Bleaching action (b) Converting ultraviolet light to visible light (c) Removing grease (d) Reflecting more white light

483. Sea water, on the average, contains 3% salt. The saltiest sea in the world contains 7.2% salt. Can you identify it?
(a) The yellow sea near China (b) The Dead Sea (c) The Caspian Sea near the Ural Mountains (d) The Coral Sea near Australia

484. The differential is a load-bearing part of a motor vehicle. Heavy loads and high

temperatures produce tremendous heat in the differentials of cars. Therefore, lubricants have been developed to withstand extreme pressures. They contain compounds of sulphur, chlorine, phosphorous and lead. These form layers of film that prevent the metal of the differential from:
(a) Rusting (b) Breaking (c) Welding (d) Bending

485. Alums used for purifying water are chemically:
(a) Sulphates of aluminium (b) Double sulphates (c) Double chlorides (d) Hydrated nitrates

486. Urea is a well known fertilizer. It is also an important material for manufacturing many items, some of which are mentioned here. Can you pick the false one?
(a) Glues (b) Plastics (c) Nylon (d) Drugs

487. Face powders are used for a smooth appearance of the skin by covering any unwanted secretions of oil. Which is the main ingredient of face powder?
(a) Zinc oxide (b) Talc (c) Precipitated chalk (d) Zinc stearate

488. Modern photography began with the Kodak Camera in 1887. This camera could take 100 pictures using a photographic film

made of cellulose nitrate. The inventor was:

(a) Kodak (b) Becquerel (c) Fox Talbot
(d) George Eastman

489. A small amount of manganese metal added to iron gives it elasticity and high tensile strength. Such steel is used in making:

(a) Boxes (b) Almirahs (c) Wheel axles
(d) Springs

490. The planets that revolve around the sun hold a special fascination for sky-loving people. The triumphant discoveries of several new elements of matter have been linked to the names of planets. Which of the following planets does not have an element named after it?

(a) Jupiter (b) Uranus (c) Neptune
(d) Pluto

491. Each of us has come from a parent father and a parent mother whose features we share, but do not look exactly like them. A clone is an exact replica of one parent, either a mother or a father. Clone frogs have actually been made, but claims of human clones have not been proved so far. What is the basis for cloning living forms of matter?

(a) All genes are identical (b) Both the single strands of DNA (genetic material) can come from one parent (c) The genes of one parent are changed to look like those of the other parent (d) The complete genetic characteristics of one parent are fed into a computer and special genes are prepared

492. The quantum theory is a suggestion that heat, light, electricity or any other form of energy:
(a) Is continuous (b) Exists in discrete bundles (c) Can be of any size (d) Is transferred in as small an amount as one could imagine

493. Lead metal is used as a covering for cables because it is not easily corroded. Since it is soft, a metal is added for hardening it. Can you identify it?
(a) Calcium (b) Iron (c) Cobalt (d) Nickel

494. Element number 61 is not found in nature. It was found among hundreds of different nuclear particles formed during the fission of uranium. It was named after the Greek mythological character who stole fire from the Gods for man. Can you identify him?
(a) Apollo (b) Hermes (c) Prometheus (d) Venus

495. Bromine in a reddish-brown liquid that can severely corrode the skin. In industry, it is used in making many things. Can you pick the false one?
(a) Petrol additives (b) Important chemicals for medicines (c) Photographic chemicals (d) Textiles

496. In the upper layers of the earth, that is, in the crust, the most abundant metal is:
(a) Iron (b) Copper (c) Zinc (d) Aluminium

497. When urea fertilizer is added, it is quickly broken down by the enzyme urease present in soil. Chemicals, called inhibitors are added to prevent urease from attacking and reducing the efficiency of urea. Which of the following is not an urease inhibitor?
(a) Phenols (b) Quinones (c) Benzene (d) Benzoquinones

498. Calcium is a mineral nutrient in the body. By adding small amounts of radioactive calcium to the body, it has been discovered that the calcium contained in the bones is:
(a) Fixed throughout life (b) Replaced by fresh calcium from the blood (c) Different from the calcium of the blood (d) Also radioactive

499. We need fresh air for breathing. Some natural sources that cause pollution of air are mentioned here. Can you pick the false one?
(a) Volcanoes (b) High-speed winds and dust storms (c) Coal fires (d) Forest fires

500. Matter can be separated into various chemicals and purified by the methods mentioned here. Which of the following is

a physico-chemical method of separation
or purification?
(a) Filtration through a filtering medium
(b) Distillation in a flask or a big tower
(c) Electrolysis (d) Leaching

Section 6

501. Radiation emitted by radioactive isotopes
can be very harmful. They are, therefore,
transported carefully in:
(a) Magnetic bottles (b) Containers made
of lead (c) Cooled helium (d) Containers
made of iron amalgam

502. Silica gel is a very useful:
(a) Wetting agent (b) Drying agent (c) Raw
material for soap (d) Solvent

503. Iron pipes are used for carrying water or
as conduits for wires of electrical fittings.
They are heavy, rust easily and are difficult
to bend. Instead of these, a lighter material
is used that does not rust and can be bent
by heating. Can you identify the material?
(a) PVC (or polyinyl chloride) (b) RCC
(c) Orlon (d) Polystyrene

504. Smoke, dust and clouds are aerosols. These
aerosols consist of gas absorbed on solid
matter consisting of fine particles. When
these fine particles absorb toxic gases, they
can be very bad for health because of their
high surface area. One kilo of coal when

dispersed as finely divided particles in an aerosol, can have a surface area equivalent to:
(a) A chess-board (b) 100 square feet of a room (c) 100 square yards of a garden (d) 1000 acres of land

505. Chlorine destroys germs. It has, therefore, many uses. Can you pick the false one?
(a) Cleaning swimming pools (b) Cleaning water for drinking (c) Cleaning water for washing utensils (d) Cleaning rust

506. The only way to travel down to a depth of 8 Kms. below the ocean surface is in a special diving craft, the bathyscaphe. Even a submarine would get crushed at this depth. A bathyscaphe uses a combination of three different materials to travel up or down. Can you pick the false one?
(a) Water from the ocean enters the chamber and the diving craft sinks (b) Cooling of petrol at a lower depth shrinks it and allows in more water (c) Iron ballast shots are released to slow descent, or, for ascent (d) Air is released at high pressure to increase the rate of ascent:

507. Aluminium chloride is used in organic chemical reactions as a catalyst. A well-know example of this is the:
(a) Grignard synthesis (b) Markownikoff addition (c) Friedel-Crafts reaction (d) Pinacolone rearrangement

508. A cigarette soaked and wetted with liquid oxygen burns:
(a) With a slow, blue flame (b) With a cold flame (c) Like a firework (d) Starting from the centre

509. Uranium, a natural radioactive element decays to form other radioactive elements and ultimately stabilizes as a non-radioactive form of:
(a) Thorium (b) Iron (c) Zinc (d) Lead

510. Lighter gases diffuse faster and can quickly fill a room. Which among the following is the lightest and diffuses the fastest?
(a) Chlorine (b) Ammonia (c) Nitrogen (d) Oxygen

511. Increasing use of fuels, like oil and coal has led to an increase in carbon dioxide. Since infrared light is partly trapped by carbon dioxide in the air, this leads to a rise in the temperature of the earth's surface, known as:
(a) The infrared effect (b) The greenhouse effect (c) A chemical effect (d) An acid rain

512. The ester of lauric acid is a low-melting solid that easily becomes an oil. Soaps made from it are very soluble in water and form a lather even with sea water. Can you identify this oil?
(a) Coconut oil (b) Olive oil (c) Cottonseed oil (d) Neem oil

513. Some substances dissolve in water in negligible quantities like one part in a million parts of water. Even glass dissolves in a very, very minute quantity in water. This tiny presence of a substance dissolved in water can be detected by:

(a) The heavier weight of water (b) A magnetic field (c) Adding a radioactive form of the substance (d) Measuring the change in the boiling point of water

514. Magnesium metal burns with a brilliant-white flame. Advantage has been taken of this property of the metal in the ways mentioned here. Can you pick the false one ?

(a) In photographic flash bulbs (b) In theatrical lighting (c) In military signal flares (d) In fireworks display

515. Iron is the most widely used metal. Some of its ores are mentioned here. Can you pick the false one?

(a) Haematite (b) Magnetite (c) Iron pyrites (d) Garnierite

516. Fruit trees like pineapple, orange and lemon, can become very short in height due to low absorption of phosphorous, when nurseries are disinfected with:

(a) Carbon dioxide gas (b) Methyl bromide gas (c) Dilute acid spray (d) A solution of chlorine

517. The Nobel Prize for medicine was awarded, in 1908, to:
(a) Paul Ehrlich for chemotherapy
(b) Louis Pasteur for the study of rabies
(c) Fleming for the discovery of pencillin
(d) Albrecht Kossel for research in proteins and cell chemistry

518. When a big, coloured balloon filled with helium rises higher into the upper layer of the atmosphere, it swells to become even bigger in size because:
(a) The plastic of the balloon becomes thin
(b) Of the cold weather at the top (c) The clouds are left far below (d) The pressure of air is less at a height

519. Powerful forces abound in Nature, many of which are still unknown. Which among the following is the strongest, natural force?
(a) Electrical force (b) Magnetic force
(c) Gravitational force (d) Nuclear force

520. From a study of the visible spectrum of hydrogen gas, it has been found that it exists in two different forms which are based on the direction of spin of the:
(a) Molecule of hydrogen (b) Atoms of the hydrogen molecule (c) Nucleii of the hydrogen atoms (d) Electrons of hydrogen

521. Polymers are often gigantic molecules consisting of long chains of repeating chemical

units. Which of the following is not a polymer?
(a) Protein (b) Cellulose (c) Rubber (d) Glucose

522. A ball rolls down the hill. A chemical reaction takes place producing heat and an explosion. These are examples of:
(a) Reversible processes (b) Irreversible processes (c) Unnatural processes (d) Simple processes

523. Manufacture of ammonia from nitrogen and hydrogen is the most widely used process in the fertiliser industry. Some facts are mentioned here. Can you pick the false one?
(a) It requires low temperatures (b) It needs high pressure (c) The reaction gives heat (d) An iron-aluminium catalyst is used

524. Radioactive substances have been decaying and releasing energy and radiation on the earth:
(a) Since the last thousand years (b) Before the universe was created (c) Since a million years (d) Since the formation of the earth

525. Underground railways provide cheap transport in metropolitan cities all over the world. Which gas is used for disinfecting the air in underground railways?
(a) Oxygen (b) Chlorine (c) Ozone (d) Carbon dioxide

526. The milk protein of which cheese is made is soft. If this protein is chemically treated, it forms a hard polymer. These hardened proteins have been used for making:
(a) Sewing needles (b) Buttons and combs
(c) Surgical thread (d) Knives and forks

527. Chelating agents can chemically bind metals in a claw-like grip to form complexes that are soluble in water. By making use of this property, it is possible to remove poisonous lead from the human body. The chelating agent used for this purpose are/is
(a) Porphyrins (b) EDTA (Ethylenediamine tetra-acetic acid) (c) Ethylenediamine (d) Ter-pyridine

528. Food articles like milk, vegetables and bread are kept in a refrigerator. Medicines are labelled 'Store in a cool, dry place'. By keeping at low temperatures, they are prevented from decay or destruction, because:
(a) Vitamins protect protein (b) Chemical reactions slow down (c) Bacteria are frozen (d) Water forms ice-crystals

529. Natural sources of radioactive minerals in nuclear reactors for generating electricity are found in limited quantities in the world. Which of the following radioactive elements is relatively more abundantly available in India?

(a) Uranium (b) Heavy water (c) Thorium
(d) Radium

530. Metals rust when they come in contact with oxygen of the air that forms oxides and thereby destroys the metal. Which metal forms an oxide with oxygen, that protects it from further rusting?
(a) Iron (b) Zinc (c) Aluminium (d) Copper

531. Shortages have resulted in the diversion of alcohol from sugarcane cultivation as a substitute for:
(a) Cold drinks in Saharan Africa (b) Petrol for dry-cleaning in Australia (c) Petrol for cars in Brazil (d) Vinegar for pickles in Italy

532. Breeder reactors are nuclear reactors that can convert non-radioactive isotopes into a radioactive, fissionable form that can be used for generating energy. Uranium-238, a non-radioactive isotope can be converted in a breeder reacter into radioactive:
(a) Uranium-234 (b) Plutonium-94
(c) Iodine-131 (d) Carbon-13

533. Radioactive isotopes are being used for medical and diagnostic applications. Iodine-131 is a radioactive form of iodine that is very useful. Some of its applications are mentioned here. Can you pick the false one?

(a) In the diagnosis of liver and kidney diorders (b) In the treatment of thyroid desease (c) For locating tumours in the brain (d) For increasing absorption of calcium in the body

534. Bell-metal is the metal used for making bells for churches. This metal gives the bell its special, ringing sound. It contains:
(a) Nickel and zinc (b) Iron and lead (c) Copper and tin (d) Silver and antimony

535. Outdoor recreation classes in public schools in Los Angeles (U.S.A.) are cancelled on those days when the:
(a) Day is warm (b) Ozone level reaches 0.35 ppm (c) There is a fast wind (d) There is a cold day and the temperature is below 10°C

536. In colour photography, the colour film is developed by oxidation of the developer and then reacting with:
(a) An acid to form a salt (b) A coupler to form a dye (c) An alkali to form a salt (d) A metal to form a pigment

537. When sugar is treated with sulphuric acid, we get a very pure form of:
(a) Water (b) Oxygen (c) Carbon (d) Hydrogen

538. Which of the following is a powerful sedative made from acetaldehyde?

(a) Acetic anhydride (b) Paraldehyde
(c) Carboxylic acids (d) L.S.D.

539. Matter on earth is composed of more than a hundred elements. If these were to be broadly divided into two groups, metals and non-metals, then how many non-metallic elements do we have on earth?
(a) 80 (b) 55 (c) 30 (d) 15

540. Which of the following materials can make cloth fire-proof?
(a) Nickel chloride (b) Aluminium sulphate
(c) Copper oxide (d) Magnesium sulphate

541. Chemical reactions often take place by collisions between molecules or atoms. But every collision need not result in chemical change. In order to react, a molecule at the time of collision must have a minimum energy known as the:
(a) Kinetic energy (b) Adiabatic heat
(c) Activation energy (d) Free energy

542. Which of the following metals is a liquid at room temperature?
(a) Iron (b) Tantalum (c) Mercury
(d) Potassium

543. Iodine-128 is a radioactive form of the same iodine that is used in tincture iodine used as a disinfectant for cuts on the skin. Iodine-128 does not have thereapeutic value because it decays quickly and loses

its radioactivity. Iodine-131, on the other hand, decays slowly. The rate of decay of radioactive substances is indicated in terms of:

(a) The total time taken for complete elimination of radioactivity (b) The number of rays emitted in one day (c) The rate at which the colour of glass is changed by radiation (d) The time taken for half the material to decay

544. Exchange of cations (positively charged particles of metals) is an important process in Nature. Can you pick the false one?
(a) In determining the fertility of soil (b) In absorbing oxygen in the soil (c) In purifying water that percolates through the soil (d) In correcting the acidity of soil

545. The glass bulb of electric bulbs becomes black due to the deposition of vapour from the:
(a) Gas in the bulb (b) Metal filament (c) Glass of the bulb (d) Joint in the glass

546. Wood is a source of some things mentioned here. Can you pick the false one?
(a) Ethyl alcohol (b) Methyl alcohol (c) Wood charcoal (d) Wood tar

547. Phenobarbitone is a sleep-inducing drug. It is also used in making:
(a) Alcohol (b) Soap (c) Acetylene (d) Urea

548. The sweet smell of roses is now available in some synthetic chemicals where similar smells have been imitated. The rose odour in these, comes from an ester formed by the reaction between formic acid and:
(a) Turpentine oil (b) Geraniol (c) Olives (d) Pine oil

549. Streptomycin is a chemical drug that is effective in the treatment of tuberculosis, meningitis and pneumonia. It was isolated from a bacterial culture by:
(a) Sir Alexander Fleming in 1946 (b) Dr. Waksman in 1944 (c) George Hevsey in 1945 (d) Flory in 1947

550. Cement sets better with water and hardens well on dampening because the material that gives hardness to cement consists of:
(a) Stable salts (b) Hydrated salts (c) Water-absorbing stone (d) Particles of sand

551. Railway steam engines convert heat from burning coal into work, but they are not 100% efficient in utilizing this heat. Their efficiency depends on their own temperature (that of steam from the boiler) and the:
(a) Presure of air (b) Temperature of the surrounding air (c) Speed of revolution of the engine (d) Fuel they consume

552. The paint industry is developing better and more sophisticated paints every year to

improve quality. A paint nowadays contains many different things. Only the basic components of a paint are mentioned here. Can you pick the false one?
(a) It contains a pigment for colour (b) The paint has a vehicle or medium like a solvent (c) A scratch-resistant polymer (d) A binder that fixes

553. Which drug given to pregnant mothers considering it was safe, resulted in the birth of deformed babies without arms or legs or shortened limbs in many countries?
(a) Streptomycin (b) Tetracycline (c) Thalidomide (d) Salicylic acid

554. One atom of the element carbon can join with another carbon atom to form long chains. This makes the chemistry of living matter unique. Which of the following elements has similar potential?
(a) Iron (b) Oxygen (c) Silicon (d) Bromine

555. Ethanol is denatured (made unfit for human consumption) by adding a poisonous substance. Can you identify it?
(a) Acetic acid (b) Methyl alcohol (c) Tartaric acid (d) Stearic acid

556. When petrol is filled in tanks at petrol-pumps and stations by petrol tankers, the petrol gets contaminated by particles of copper metal released from the tubes and

piping of copper into the petrol passing through. Some copper contamination comes from the copper parts of the motor vehicle engine using the petrol. Therefore, anti-oxidants are added to prevent the copper from making the engine 'knock' and from forming sticky gum that blocks the carburettor. Some of these antioxdants are mentioned here. Can you pick the false one?
(a) Phenylenediamine (b) Aminophenols (c) Nitrobenzene (d) Ortho-alkylated phenols

557. Glass is a transparent substance obtained by heating white sand with metal oxides or carbonates. It is a mixture of:
(a) Chlorides (b) Phosphates (c) Sulphates (d) Silicates

558. Tennis balls are made by placing a pellet of sodium nitrite and ammonium chloride, each, in the two halves of the ball which are then sealed. When these pellets react, they release a gas which expands the tennis ball. Can you identify the gas?
(a) Ammonia (b) Nitrogen (c) Hydrogen chloride (d) Chlorine

559. Ordinary gasoline (petrol) that is used as fuel for cars, scooters and automobiles contains many different chemicals that are added in small quantities, each performing an important role. Some of these are

mentioned here. Can you pick the false one?

(a) Anti-rust agents for protecting against corrosion by water (b) Anti-icing agents for depressing the freezing point of particles of ice (c) Soaps for removing particles of grease from petrol tanks ensure a free flow of petrol (d) Detergents for preventing gums from sticking on the walls of the carburettor

560. When chalk was mixed with silver nitrate and exposed to light, it was observed that it became dark. This marked the beginning of:

(a) Colour television (b) The Polaroid camera (c) Black and white photography (d) The Video camera

561. Through the body of every person, millions of tiny particles pass through silently every second. Can you identify these particles here?

(a) Protons (b) Neutrinos (c) Electrons (d) Atoms

562. When two compounds have the same chemical formula, (that is, they have the same number and variety of atoms) but have different linkages between atoms and hence different properties, they are called:

(a) Allotropes (b) Isomorphs (c) Isomers (d) Isotopes

563. Noble gases are inert, that is, under normal conditions they do not react. Which of the following is not a noble gas?
(a) Helium (b) Lithium (c) Neon (d) Argon

564. 'Baked-on paints' are alkyd resins which are very tough, cross-linked polymers, used as a finishing for cars, jeeps, refrigerators and stoves. The word 'alkyd' means:
(a) Alcohol baked (b) Alkaline derivative (c) Alcohol and acid (d) A low-key distemper

565. One ounce of gold can be drawn into a wire:
(a) Six inches long (b) Ten feet long (c) One mile long (d) Fifty miles long

566. Dirty water contains germs and can be harmful. Swimming pools are disinfected by bubbling through water a controlled amount of:
(a) Bromine (b) Oxygen (c) Air (d) Chlorine

567. Which of the following cannot be dissolved in alcohol?
(a) Resins and varnishes (b) Soaps and varnishes (c) Dyes and drugs (d) Rubber and plastics

568. By measuring the radiation emitted by radioactive substances added to blood, we can find out its volume. Which of the

following radioactive isotopes have been used for measuring the volume of blood?
(a) Tritium (b) Iodine-131 (c) Carbon-13 (d) Uranium-238

569. Electron microscopes are very powerful instruments that can form images of the tiniest micro-structures by generating waves:
(a) Of light to see electrons (b) On a radium-coated screen (c) Of electrons that are smaller than the waves of light (d) X-rays that are smaller than the tiniest matter

570. Cement binds bricks and stones very hard and is used as a building material where strength is required like, in roofs, pillars and multi-storied structures. Cement is essentially, a complex mixture of calcium:
(a) Silicates and aluminates (b) Oxides and carbonates (c) Permanganates and sul-phates (d) Hydrides and hydrates

571. Electrical energy can be converted, almost completely, into work. According to the Second Law of Thermodynamics, heat (a form of energy) is partly converted into useful work and part of it:
(a) Becomes electrical energy (b) Is always wasted (c) Becomes magnetism (d) Increases the weight of the body

572. Ocean-going vessels are not able to utilize sea water for drinking purposes because it

contains salt. On applying pressure on sea water contained in a tank, pure water flows out through a semipermeable membrane of cellulose acetate,leaving salt behind. This method of obtaining fresh water from sea water is known as:

(a) Osmosis (b) Filtration (c) Reverse osmosis (d) Pressure desalination

573. The high energy and speed of turbo-jet racing cars has been accomplished by a technical modification which provides extra energy from:

(a) The faster burning of petrol (b) A faster electric current from the battery (c) The heat of the exhaust (escaping) gases (d) The frictional heat energy produced by tyres on the road surface

574. In the last quarter of the eighteenth century it was noticed that people who cleaned fire-chimneys in England had a higher rate of skin-cancer which was due to a chemical found in coal-dust in 1933. Can you identify it?

(a) Cresols (b) Benzopyrene (c) Toluene (d) Salicylic acid

575. Soaps remove dirt by forming a chemical link between:

(a) Water and the particles of dirt (b) Two small particles of dirt (c) Ten particles of dirt (d) Dirt particles and oxygen in the air

576. When pure lime is used for whitewashing the walls of a building, it is unable to protect them. A weather-resistant, hard film of cross-linked polymer can be made for the walls, by adding in the presence of formaldehyde:
(a) Soap (b) Large crystals of sugar (c) Skimmed milk (d) Coconut oil

577. When wire glass is hit, it prevents pieces of glass from falling or spreading after breaking. Wire glass contains:
(a) Cobalt (b) A sheet of nylon net (c) A network of steel wire (d) A sheet of fibre glass

578. Volatile compounds of boron burn with a:
(a) Red flame (b) Blue flame (c) Green flame (d) Orange-red flame

579. Which of the following elements can be toxic to plants growing in soils that are high in acidity?
(a) Nitrogen (b) Copper (c) Iron (d) Aluminium

580. Silver bromide, a chemical used in photography, is found in:
(a) India (b) Germany (c) South America (d) Japan

581. When a solid crystal is melted, it should become a liquid. Liquid crystals are an intermediate stage between a liquid and a

crystal. Which of the following is a liquid crystal of a non-living system?
(a) Striated muscle fibre (b) Axons of nerve cells (c) Cholesteryl bromide (d) Cilia

582. Glass thermometers are made by coating the glass with wax and then etching, that is, cutting lines and numbers on the glass with:
(a) Sulphuric acid (b) Caustic soda (c) A fine metal cutter (d) Hydrofluoric acid

583. Beryl is the main ore of the light metal:
(a) Lithium (b) Beryllium (c) Magnesium (d) Boron

584. There is a worldwide demand for aluminium metal, which is being manufactured in great quantities. Which of the following is incorrect about its process of manufacture?
(a) The raw material used is bauxite (b) Molten cryolite is added (c) A relatively, low temperature is maintained (d) A huge electric current is passed

585. The world is facing an energy crisis. Of the alternative sources of energy, there is only one which offers an almost limitless supply by fusing together two small atoms on a commercial scale. The raw material required for this is:
(a) Radioactive uranium ore (b) Refined sand from deserts and beaches (c) Water from oceans, rivers and lakes (d) Air

586. Coloured glass is made by adding the oxide of a metal. This gives rise to a silicate. From different metal oxides we get differently coloured glass. Can you pick the false one?
(a) Blue glass (from cobalt oxide) (b) Yellow glass (from aluminium oxide) (c) Green glass (from ferrous oxide) (d) Red glass (from copper oxide)

587. For studying chemical reactions at a high pressure, proper materials are required, otherwise the containers will break. Which of the following is used in the construction of high-pressure vessels?
(a) Duralumin (b) High-speed steel (c) Carboloy (d) Cobalt-nickel alloy

588. Hydrogen forms a 'bridge' in the chemical structure of which of the following?
(a) Ice (b) Diborane (c) Hydrogen peroxide (d) Lithium hydride

589. When the artificial chemical element number 101 was made, the quantity available was so small that only four atoms could be identified by scientists using advanced techniques for detection of small particles. The element was named in honour of:
(a) Otto Hahn, the father of the hydrogen bomb (b) Mendeleev, the father of the modern periodic table of chemical elements (c) Einstein, the father of the theory of

Relativity (d) Madame Curie, the renowned scientist

590. Cement is formed by burning in a hot kiln: (a) Chalk and graphite (b) Limestone and graphite (c) Limestone and clay (d) Sulphur and limestone

591. A plant by the name of Clarckia Pulchellu, when fully grown, but before bursting, contains grains of pollen of a very small size - 5,000 times smaller than an inch. Brown found that these fine grains moved in water just in the same manner in which particles of soot or dust moved in the air around London, that were:
(a) Molecules (b) Atoms (c) Crystals (d) Colloids

592. Sometimes the behaviour of a chemical compound can be better understood by regarding it as if it exists in a world between two or more different possible structures. This phenomena is called:
(a) Isomerism (b) Allotropism (c) A double standard (d) Resonance

593. Coal was formed under high temperature and pressure from:
(a) Marine matter (b) Burnt rocks and clay (c) Black rock and iron (d) Giant forests and vegetable matter

594. Which of the following is not a mineral containing aluminium oxide?

(a) Corundum (b) Rutile (c) Bauxite
(d) Emery

595. Even after it is removed, gold leaves a trace
wherever it is kept such as on a piece of
cloth. Crime detectives can tell the carat or
purity of missing gold that has been stolen
from the:
(a) Purity of gold present in the trace left
on the cloth (b) Percentage of impurities
in the trace of gold (c) Heavier weight of
cloth containing the trace of gold (d) Signals from detective dogs

596. Scientists say that there are 'black holes' in
the universe swallowing matter. Others
speak of 'white holes' creating and spewing
out millions of tons of matter. The steady-
state school of scientific thinkers believe
that:
(a) There are as many white holes as black
ones (b) Matter is created and swallowed
in equal quantities (c) 'Black holes' and
'white holes' are mirror universes (d) When
a 'black hole' meets a 'white hole', both
vanish

597. When William Perkins the scientist was a
young man he was trying to make quinine
(a drug). He discovered, instead:
(a) Mauveine, a violet, synthetic dye
(b) Oxalic acid (c) Bakelite, a plastic
(d) Nitroglycerine, an explosive

598. Temporary and permanent hardness in water can be both removed by adding:
(a) Potash (b) Sodium carbonate (c) A few drops of lemon juice (d) Salt

599. A solution of chromium oxide in concentrated sulphuric acid is used for cleaning glass in laboratories because it:
(a) Dissolves glass (b) Oxidises grease (c) Removes sand particles (d) Reacts with dust

600. Silver is a precious metal used in jewellery and in industry. It is found in certain ores mentioned here. Can you pick the false one?
(a) Argentite (b) Ruby silver (c) Horn silver (d) Siderite

Section 7

601. Large deposits of sulphur are found in some places. Can you pick the false one?
(a) Sicily (b) France (c) United States (d) Japan

602. Beneath the surface of the ocean, there is no air available for burning fuel. Which of the following chemicals is used with oil as an underwater fuel?
(a) Hydrogen (b) Hydrogen peroxide (c) Sulphuric acid (d) Magnesium

603. When primitive man added tin to copper, he obtained bronze, an alloy, that was harder than copper and therefore more useful as a weapon and an agricultural tool. The making of bronze started as early as: (a) 500 B.C. (b) 1,500 B.C. (c) 3,000 B.C. (d) One million B.C.

604. A hundred years ago, efforts were made to find a substitute for expensive ivory of the elephant tusk, used in the white balls of the indoor game, billiards. This led to the invention of: (a) The cloth dacron (b) Polyester yarn (c) The plastic, celluloid (d) Polythene plastic

605. When basic cations like sodium, calcium and magnesium are leached out in humid places by the action of water: (a) Alkaline soils are formed (b) Acidic soils are formed (c) Stiff soils are formed (d) The soil level declines

606. If a tennis ball is placed in an air-tight box and the lid is closed, then, if anyone asks "where is the ball?" we reply, "It is somewhere in the box". But if the ball was an electron, nobody would be sure whether it would be inside the box or outside it. This unusual behaviour of the electron (a tiny particle of the atom) is known as the: (a) Rolling ball (b) Tunnel effect (c) Outside behaviour (d) Magic trick

607. Colouring of finger nails or toe nails has been a traditional form of beauty in many places. Use of nail polish has become popular, worldwide. It contains many things. Which of the following is not a part of nail polish?
(a) Nitroceullulse, which gives a shining film to nail polish (b) A protein makes this film less brittle (c) A resin is added that makes the nail polish stick to the nail (d) Acetone is used as a solvent that dissolves the ingredients

608. Which of the following metals, when added to steel, makes it suitable for cutting purposes by maintaining the 'cutting edge' of the blade?
(a) Manganese (b) Vanadium (c) Lithium (d) Potassium

609. Gold paint is made from:
(a) Gold (b) Platinum (c) Copper (d) Antimony

610. When petrol burns in an engine, the gases leaving the ignition chamber of the engine may contain glowing particles that may ignite fresh fuel entering the engine. To prevent the glow of these particles, tricresyl phosphate (TCP) is added, which also prevents leakage of current caused by deposits on the spark plugs. This additive to petroleum is known as:

(a) An anti-knocking agent (b) A lubricant
(c) A deposit modifier (d) An anti-oxidant

611. Limestone is a white rock consisting mainly
of one mineral, calcite. Some of the industrial uses of limestone are mentioned
here. Can you pick the false one?
(a) In the extraction of iron from its ore
(b) In making soda and glass (c) For
making cement (d) In the extraction of tin

612. Normal butane and iso-butane are gases
which have the same number of hydrogen
and carbon atoms in their molecules (smallest, independently existing particles), but
boil at different temperatures, because:
(a) Normal butane is more hot (b) Their
volumes are different (c) Iso-butane is an
acid (d) Their atoms do not have the same
arrangement in space

613. Plywood sheets are stuck together by un-
polymerised:
(a) Urea-formaldehyde resins (b) Carbon
black (c) Nylon (d) Styrene and butadiene

614. At a suitable pressure near the freezing
point of ice, we can have:
(a) Only ice (b) Ice and water only (c) Ice
and steam, existing together only (d) Ice,
water and steam, all existing side by side

615. 'Mutation' means alteration of a gene,
which is a biochemical substance in the

body that determines hereditary characterstics such as height or the colour of eyes. Which of the following is not a cause of gene mutation?
(a) Ultraviolet radiation (b) Effect of chemicals (c) Cold temperatures (d) Effect of radioactive material

616. The electric batteries used in small calculators are:
(a) Nickel-cadmium batteries (b) Leclanche cell (c) Weston cell (d) Lead acid batteries

617. Which of the following chemicals has caused disasters by exploding in the holds of ships in harbours and in warehouses?
(a) Gold chloride (b) Ammonium nitrate
(c) Vinegar in bottles under pressure
(d) Caustic soda

618. A lot of controversy has been generated over the use of 'BVO' in soft drinks on the ground that it is carcinogenic (cancer-causing). What is 'BVO'?
(a) B-complex vitamin overdose (b) Basic vitamin overdose (c) Brominated vegetable oil (d) Bakery vanilla odour

619. Fine wire is drawn through diamonds, for making:
(a) Electrical conductors (b) Springs for watches (c) Copper wire for motor coils (d) Fine embroidery

620. Safety glass is used in windshields of motor vehicles as it protects against injury. It is made by binding together layers of:
(a) Soft and hard glass (b) Glass with glue (c) Glass and plastic (d) Mica and glass

621. Formic acid is the smallest organic acid with a carboxyl group. Some of its uses in industry are mentioned here. Can you pick the false one?
(a) In the dyeing industry (b) In making industrial alcohol (c) In bleaching of textiles (d) In electro-plating

622. Many hydrocarbons that are obtained from petroleum are made of molecules that have the shape of straight chains. By converting them into hydrocarbons having the scattered structured of a tree-branch, the 'knocking' sound from a motor car engine is reduced. This conversion is known as:
(a) Cracking (b) Reforming (c) Lean gas formation (d) Refining

623. Greeks and Egyptians, in ancient times, were familiar with the use of alum as:
(a) A paint for wood (b) A preservative (c) A cream (d) A mordant for dyeing fabric

624. Cheese from Switzerland contains blowholes. While making steel, similar blowholes are created by oxygen. Which metal

is added to molten steel for combining with oxygen and preventing bubbles?
(a) Copper (b) Nickel (c) Manganese (d) Tungsten

625. Photography began in the ninteenth century when Herschel found that it was possible to dissolve silver chloride, a photosensitive material in:
(a) Vinegar (b) Alcohol (c) Sodium thiosulphate (d) Potassium permanganate

626. Police crime detectives make an impression of the track of a motor vehicle tyre on a mould made from:
(a) Lycopodium powder (b) Plaster of Paris (c) Quick-drying clay (d) Wax

627. Sodium cyanide is used in the:
(a) Purification of acids (b) Creation of fires (c) Cleaning of silver (d) Extraction of gold

628. Biological molecules are a world in themselves. While photographing the complex, giant Vitamin B-12 molecule, using X-rays:
(a) Layers of it may be sliding away (b) It may be breaking up into many molecules (c) Streams of water, one molecule thin may be passing through it (d) There may be fats and proteins being made inside it

629. Nuclear power reactors that supply energy have to operate at low temperatures and

consequently with a lower efficiency because:

(a) The nuclear heat is carried by ordinary steam (b) It is difficult to heat uranium (c) The walls of the nuclear containers cannot withstand higher temperatures (d) The high pressure inside the reactor reduces the temperature

630. Radium emits radiation and is therefore called a radioactive element. Traces of this element are found in some ores mentioned here. Can you pick the false one?
(a) Ores of uranium in Europe (b) Ores of uranium in parts of Russia (c) Ores of lead in Brazil (d) Carnotite ore in the U.S.A.

631. Industrial hydrogen is manufactured by passing an electric current through a solution of:
(a) Carbon dioxide (b) Sodium hydroxide (c) Alumina (d) Magnesium hydroxide

632. In Japan the seaweed, *Laminaria Japonica*, had been used for hundreds of years to improve the flavour of food. Nowadays, it is used as 'Ajinomoto', a white, flavouring powder used in Chinese food, like, in noodles. What is 'Ajinomoto'?
(a) Sodium chloride (b) Monosodium glutamate (an amino acid) (c) Palmitic acid (a fat) (d) Lactase (an enzyme)

633. Efforts have been made to try and find out what the earth was like billions of years ago. It is believed that about 3 billion years ago:
(a) There was no air (b) There was no oxygen in the air (c) There was no carbon dioxide (d) There was life on earth

634. Alcohol is sometimes used in:
(a) Baking powder (b) Weighing instruments (c) Thermometers (d) Paints

635. Some substances are commonly used for removing acidic gases. Which of the following is commonly used in the chemical industry for removal of hydrogen sulphide from coal gas?
(a) Quick lime (b) Slaked lime (c) Milk of magnesia (d) Sodium hydride

636. Which of the following is not an alloy containing tin metal?
(a) Bronze for statues (b) Pewter for hardness (c) Solder for soldering electrical contacts (d) Brass for articles like bangles and utensils:

637. Sodium hypochlorite, a laundry bleaching agent, is used for bleaching clothes. However, it has a disadvantage, that it reacts with nitrogen of peptide chemical bonds. Therefore, it should not be used for bleaching:

(a) Terylene (b) Cotton (c) Wool
(d) Polyester

638. Mortar used in joining bricks is a mixture of water, slaked lime and sand. When it sets hard, the lime is slowly converted into calcium carbonate by:
(a) Reaction of the lime with sand (b) Carbon dioxide from the air (c) Reaction of lime with water (d) The pressure of bricks on the lime

639. Lead forms many paint materials. Which paint material made of lead is highly resistant to corrosion by water?
(a) Red lead (b) White lead (c) Litharge (d) Lead sulphide

640. Ozone is a rare gas found in the outer reaches of the atmosphere. Small quantities are sometimes produced by:
(a) Heating rusted iron (b) Electric sparks of electric trains (c) Electrical heaters (d) Melting ice from glaciers

641. Spaceships have to be air-tight because in space there is no air, only vaccum. Which of the following compounds has been used for air-tight closing of the door (hatch) in lunar modules?
(a) Bakelite (b) Silicones (c) Chlorides (d) Hydro-carbons

642. The alkali metals form strong bases, salts and stable carbonates. Which of the following elements does not belong to this chemical family?
(a) Lithium (b) Sodium (c) Potassium (d) Magnesium

643. Scientists have been able to make electric fuel cells using naturally available substances. If they succeed in, using these cells in motor vehicles, transport would become very convenient. Can you guess what is the natural material used in these cells?
(a) Wood (b) Naturally-occurring ores of copper (c) Naturally-occurring ores of uranium (d) Natural gas

644. Manganese is an important metal used in the steel industry. Deposits of manganese ore are found in large quantities in the countries mentioned here. Can you pick the false one?
(a) Russia (b) India (c) United States (d) Spain

645. It is possible for a solid to get dispersed in another solid in such a fine manner that it appears to be dissolved, although it is not. The following are examples of colloidal solutions of a solid in a solid. Can you pick the false one?
(a) Black diamonds (b) Ruby glass (c) Metal alloys (d) Pumice stone used for scrubbing hands and feet

646. Many substances like paper pulp, linen and other fabrics contain colouring matter in their raw state that requires to be removed before further processing. They can be bleached by various bleaching agents. Which of the following is not a bleaching agent?
(a) Chlorine (b) Hydrogen peroxide (c) Acetic acid (d) Bleaching powder

647. Silver can be spread as a thin sheet on another metal by electroplating. The film of silver sticks strongly to the metal. Which of the following metals cannot be properly plated with silver?
(a) Nickel (b) Iron (c) Copper (d) Brass

648. On heating, sodium and sulphur can be melted. Molten sodium and molten sulphur are used:
(a) As catalysts (b) As a medium for extracting metals (c) For refining lead (d) As electrodes in a modern kind of battery

649. Scientific curiosity led to the discovery that matter was made of elements. Since there were many elements that combined with each other to form a variety of materials with different properties, it was necessary to denote the elements by symbols and numbers. The notation of elements by symbols that we used today was started by:
(a) Robert Boyle (b) Berzelius (c) Lavoisier (d) Scheele

650. Which of the following chemicals coated on photographic paper are used in photography for creating images of objects by the action of light?
(a) Copper salts (b) Silver salts (c) Sulphur acids (d) Bases of iron

651. Coins are made of special metals that do not rust, react or decay easily as they are meant to last for a long time. Which of the following metals is not known to used have been used for coins?
(a) Silver (b) Nickel (c) Tungsten (d) Gold

652. An atom of can be smashed and broken into many nuclear particles by the high acceleration (increasing speed) imparted in:
(a) An electron microscope (b) A Cyclotron (c) A Chromatograph (d) A cathode-ray tube

653. Which oxidizing agent is contained in matches, fireworks and explosives?
(a) Hydrogen peroxide (b) Potassium permanganate (c) Potassium chlorate (d) Sodium peroxide

654. Zeolites are ion-exchange resins used for softening of water. Superior ion-exchangers were made just before the Second World War. These consisted of:

(a) Finely divided silica (b) A giant structure of hydrocarbons (c) Fine sand (d) Organic salts of lithium

655. Graphite is made of atoms of carbon joined together. It is a good conductor of electricity because some of the electrons in the carbon atoms of graphite are:
(a) Attached to each other (b) Strongly linked to other carbon atoms (c) Not attached to any particular carbon atom (d) Are not free to move under an electric current

656. The explosive TNT is made from:
(a) Toluene (b) Phthalic acid (c) Thorium (d) Tin

657. Ultraviolet rays in sunlight can make the paint on your car, house doors and windows crack, de-polymerise or fade. Paint can be protected from ultraviolet light in the ways mentioned here. Can you pick the false one?
(a) By using pigments that absorb the rays (b) By using pigments that reflect the rays (c) By using oil-based pigments (d) By adding ultraviolet absorbers in the last coat of paint

658. Clays like Kaolinite, are used for making articles of pottery such as crockery, vases and toys because they:

(a) Shrink and swell with water (b) Do not shrink and swell with water (c) Are red in colour (d) Are free from impurities

659. Moulding powders of urea resin and cellulosic fillers are available in a variety of colours. They have a hard, durable surface and are used for making various articles, some of which are mentioned here. Can you pick the false one?
(a) Buttons and bottle caps (b) Display boxes (c) Bread wrappers (d) Surgical items

660. When an atom reacts chemically and gains one or more electrons, it is said to have been:
(a) Reduced (b) Oxidized (c) Catalyzed (d) Decomposed

661. When any bio-organic matter decays, it becomes a part of the earth (soil), a part of the air and a part of water. This works like a law of nature for traditional waste. But chemical industry is finding it difficult to make chemicals that are not toxic to the environment and can be easily broken down by bacteria in the air, soil or water. Which of the following chemicals is not 'biodegradable'?
(a) Cellulose, a raw material of rayon industry (b) D.D.T., a pesticide (c) Sodium straight-chain alkyl benzene sulphonate, a detergent (d) Sodium citrate, an additive in detergents

662. The smallest particles that can take part in a chemical reaction are sometimes electrically charged. The chemical substances made of such particles are said to be linked by ionic bonds. Which of the following chemicals does not have an ionic bond?
(a) Sodium chloride (b) Ferric oxide (c) Sugar (d) Calcium carbonate

663. Some chemical elements have been named after the native countries of the scientists who discovered them. Can you pick the false one?
(a) Germanium from Germany (b) Gallium from France (Gaul) (c) Polonium from Poland (d) Vanadium from Venezuela

664. Synthetic petrol and kerosine can be made from coal by passing one of the following gases under heat and pressure over coal:
(a) Oxygen (b) Hydrogen (c) Nitrogen (d) Carbon dioxide

665. The atomic weight of elements is based on comparison using as a standard nowadays:
(a) Oxygen, with an atomic mass of 16
(b) Carbon, with an atomic mass of 12
(c) Hydrogen, with an atomic mass of 1
(d) Sulphur, with an atomic mass of 32

666. Almost 500 antibiotics, including streptomycin, aureomycin and terramycin have been isolated from:

(a) Alluvial soil (b) The bacteria, rhizobium (c) Kentucky bluegrass (d) The bacteria, actinomycetes

667. Tin metal has been known from ancient times. It is extracted from the ore tinstone (stannic oxide) by heating it in a furnace with:
(a) Chalk (b) Lime (c) Steam (d) Coal

668. Propylene is extracted from crude petroleum and converted into polypropylene, which is used in the making of various products, some of which are mentioned here. Can you pick the false one?
(a) Clothes (b) Ropes (c) In heat-resistant plastics (d) In parachute ropes

669. Sulphur dioxide is a major air pollutant emitted by electric power plants and metal furnaces. There are various ways by which pollution of the immediate and general environment by sulphur dioxide can be reduced. Some are mentioned here. Can you pick the false one?
(a) Increasing the height of the chimney (b) Passing ultraviolet light (c) Reacting with calcium oxide (from limestone) and precipitating by an electrostatic discharge (d) Passing sulphur dioxide through molten sodium carbonate

670. Lavoisier is known as the 'father of modern chemistry'. Some of his contributions are mentioned here. Can you pick the false one?
(a) He concluded that a substance increases or loses weight, depending on whether it combines with or loses oxygen, respectively. (b) He gave a list of twenty-five elements of matter (c) He stressed quantitative methods of chemical investigation (d) He explained that substances that can be easily burned are rich in Phlogiston

671. Non-stick frying pans are coated black with teflon, a material that is resistant to heat. Teflon is a polymer of:
(a) Ethylene (b) Styrene (c) Fluoromethane (d) Tetrafluoroethylene

672. Calcium products are used in making many important things mentioned here. Can you pick the false one?
(a) Cement (b) Washing soda (c) Drinking soda (d) Quicklime

673. Which of the following fibres is said to be very harmful for health?
(a) Hay (b) Asbestos (c) Sawdust (d) Cellulose

674. Adolf von Baeyer of Germany was awarded the Nobel Prize in 1905 for his brilliant work on studying and preparing:
(a) Textile fibres (b) Dyes (c) Steel (d) Plastic

675. Fluorocarbons are used in making various articles, some of which are mentioned here. Can you pick the false one?
(a) In gaskets (b) Conveyor belts (c) Buttons (d) Laminations

676. Ice floats on water because it has an open structure compared to water and therefore occupies a greater volume of space for the same weight. This open structure of ice is due to:
(a) Magnetic forces (b) Hydrogen bonding (c) The solid state of ice (d) The crystalline nature of ice

677. Limestone has slowly formed in the oceans over millions of years. The release of excess carbon dioxide in the oceans may disrupt this geological process by:
(a) Not participating in the making of calcium carbonate (b) Chemically, breaking up calcium carbonate (c) Converting insoluble carbonate to soluble bicarbonate. (d) Blocking the formation of calcium carbonate

678. Very fast conduction of electricity by matter is called superconductivity. This happens when matter is:
(a) Heated to high temperatures (b) Cooled to very low temperatures (c) Dissolved in acids (d) Treated with radiation

679. The wear and tear of tyres can be tested off the road in the laboratory, by rotating

the tyre at a fast speed against a hard, road-like surface and measuring the loss of:

(a) Radioactive material added to the tyre (b) Black colour of the tyre (c) Thickness of the tyre (d) Precision balance

680. Mercury can dissolve metals. These mixtures have been used for dental fillings. The metals which have been used for this are mentioned here. Can you pick the false one?

(a) Silver (b) Tin (c) Copper (d) Iron

681. Heavy snow can block traffic on roads. It is difficult to melt the ice. Which of the following melts ice on roads even at temperatures below 0°C?

(a) Zinc oxide (b) Hydrated magnesium sulphate (c) Hydrated calcium chloride (d) Bauxite

682. Potash (potassium carbonate) is used as a fertilizer. It is also known as:

(a) Pearl ash (b) Oil of vitriol (c) Azo compound (d) Glauber's salt

683. Before the birth of chemistry, there was alchemy in the West, a desire to change metals into gold for wealth. In India, the roots of chemistry lie in:

(a) The desire for Amrita, a drink believed to make one immortal (b) The quest for a touch-stone that turns everything into gold

(c) The search for a medicine that cured every illness (d) The desire to imitate the fragrance of chandan (sandalwood)

684. Many fruits have pleasant odours. Some of the pleasant odours of common fruits are due to:
(a) Alcohol (b) Sugars (c) Fats (d) Esters

685. Permanent hardness in water cannot be removed by boiling. This type of hardness is due to the presence of metal:
(a) Oxides (b) Sulphates (c) Nitrides (d) Bicarbonates

686. Alchemists, in olden times, tried to convert ordinary metal into gold or silver. In modern times, silver can be bombarded by neutrons and changed into:
(a) Copper (b) Platinum (c) Cadmium (d) Carbon

687. Zinc is used for plating metals, for roofs and fences to protect them from corrosion. This plating process, known as galvanization, was invented by the chemist:
(a) Galvani of Italy (b) Boyle of Britain (c) Scheele (d) Buchner

688. Sometimes in a hurry, we forget to mix sugar added to tea and therefore do not get a sweet taste. The speed at which a cube of sugar dissolves in a cup of tea, depends on the:

(a) Weight of the cube (b) Colour of the cube (c) Surface area of the cube (d) Sweetness of the sugar

689. A lot of money is spent on protection of buildings, bridges, utensils and appliances from rust. Some methods of protection are mentioned below. Can you pick the false one?
a) Applying grease (b) Galvanising (c) Annealing (d) Painting

690. Matter behaves differently in the tiny world of the atom. If we know more of the whereabouts of a small atomic particle like an electron, the less we know about its:
(a) Momentum (b) Colour (c) Speed (d) Electric charge

691. Mushroom is an expensive vegetable. Some mushrooms are edible, others are poisonous. Deadly toxin is contained in the mushroom having the botanical name:
(a) *Caoutchouc* (b) *Eremophilia freelingii* (c) *Amanita phalloides* (d) *Gibberella furikuroi*

692. Ammonia and Boron trifluorde are an example of:
(a) An acid-alkali pair (b) An electron donor-acceptor pair (c) A pair of isomers (d) A pair of allotropes

693. Playing with models of atoms and bonds, Francis Crick and James Watson, both Nobel Laureates, discovered that:

(a) The green colour of chlorophyll in plants is due to absorption of other colours (b) DNA of genes in the body is shaped like a double helix (c) Half the proteins in the body are linear like a string (d) Sugar is a polymer

694. Glycol is used in car radiators as:
(a) A coolant (b) A lubricant (c) An agent for high speed air-fuel mixtures (d) An anti-freeze agent

695. Carbon dioxide has many well-known uses. Can you pick the false one?
(a) In making cold drinks (aerated waters) (b) In fire extinguishers (c) In disinfecting water (d) In making sodium carbonate

696. Substances like nitrophenol, can form hydrogen bonds (loose chemical links) internally, that is, within the molecule. They, therefore, have a:
(a) Very high melting point (b) Very high viscosity (c) Low melting point (d) Yellow colour

697. Every year, bacteria help in removing 200 million tonnes of carbon dioxide that is released in the air by industries, vehicles and domestic cooking, harmful to human beings and other forms of life. Greenery belts in cities are necessary because these bacteria which help us are not present in the place mentioned here. Can you pick the false one?

(a) Under road soil (b) Under houses (c) In congested areas of cities (d) Under shaded lawns

698. Clothes are bleached by bleaching powder. This is done by dipping the fabric in a very dilute solution of bleaching powder and:
(a) Washing off the solution (b) Drying in the sun (c) Exposing to air (d) Then dipping in a common salt bath

699. Which metal can exist in a form that gives sparks on scratching?
(a) Tin (b) Lead (c) Antimony (d) Thallium

700. Desiccants are substances that react with water or moisture in the air and thus keep other substances dry. Some useful desiccants are mentioned here. Can you pick the false one?
(a) Quicklime (b) Sulphuric acid crystals (c) Anhydrides (d) Salt

Section 8

701. Those people who chew betel leaves know that gold or silver foil is used to make them look attractive and also on dishes like 'rice pulao' or 'paneer' (fried cottage cheese). A bar of gold of a thickness of one inch can be made into:

(a) Ten sheets of gold foil (b) A thousand sheets of gold foil (c) Two and a half lakh sheets of gold foil (d) Five crore sheets of gold foil

702. The world's biggest suppliers of silver are mentioned here. Can you pick the false one?
(a) Mexico (b) India (c) United States (d) Canada

703. Steel has the advantage of being stronger than iron. The art of coverting iron into steel by man is estimated to have begun as far back as:
(a) 200 B.C. (b) 1400 B.C. (c) 1800 B.C. (d) 2500 B.C.

704. Formic acid has several uses, some of which are mentioned here. Can you pick the false one?
(a) In the tanning industry (b) In textile industry (c) As a solvent for dyes (d) For coagulation of rubber latex

705. Central American Indians, in the sixteenth century, made rubber from latex, which was soft. Later, Goodyear found that rubber could be made into hard tyres by adding sulphur, which cross-linked the polymer chains of soft rubber, hardening it. This process is known as:
(a) Sulphurization (b) Tyre-beading (c) Galvanization (d) Vulcanisation

706. Which of the following acids is present in our stomach?
(a) Sulphuric acid (b) Hydrochloric acid
(c) Nitric acid (d) Pinic acid

707. The energy that is required to pull off an electron from an atom is known as the:
(a) Thermal energy (b) Ionizatin energy
(c) Magnetic potential (d) Activation energy

708. Calcium metal in a flame imparts:
(a) A blue colour (b) A greenish-blue colour (c) White light (d) An orange-red colour

709. In 1952, when the first Hydrogen-bomb was exploded on the Bikini Atoll in the Pacific, aeroplanes were sent to collect samples of nuclear fragments fallen out from the mushroom cloud of the bomb. New, artificial chemical elements were found to have been produced. Can you identify them?
(a) Uranium and Thorium (b) Radium and Polonium (c) Californium and Hahnium
(d) Einsteinium and Fermium

710. A concentrated solution of caustic soda chemically attacks glass, therefore, the container used for storing such a solution is:
(a) An iron bottle (b) A tin box with a thick glass lid (c) A polythene wrapper (d) A wax-coated glass bottle

711. Garden chairs made of plastic strips and plastic articles get faded, worn out and cracked in sunlight, mainly because of:
(a) Heat (b) Ultraviolet rays (c) Low melting point of plastic (d) The red colour

712. You can make acetylene by dropping water on:
(a) Chalk (b) Calcium carbide (c) Calcium carbonate (d) Burning coal

713. Pearlitic steels have very high strength because they contain:
(a) Pearls that are bright and hard (b) Cementite (or ferric carbide), a hard substance (c) Chromium (d) More than 26% carbon

714. Faraday discovered that an electric moving in a magnetic field could produce a current of electricity. Thus, the dynamo was invented for generating electricity which made it possible to extract various metals on a large scale, in an electric arc furnace. Some of these metals are mentioned here. Can you pick the false one?
(a) Chromium (b) Aluminium (c) Stainless steel (d) Lead

715. When caustic soda is manufactured from sea water, one of the important by-products is:
(a) Chromium (b) Chlorine (c) Potash (d) Fertilizer

716. The rough, reddish-brown strip on a safety matchbox is used for lighting a match by striking against it. It is made of powdered glass mixed with:
(a) Red lead (b) Violet phosphorous (c) Mercury (d) Potash

717. Neon and argon gases are used in luminous:
(a) Electric signboards (b) Matches (c) Firework displays (d) Festival candles

718. Ice floats on water because it is lighter. When water at the low temperature of 4°C is cooled to 0°C, it expands to form ice. This expansion of water to form ice has been used for:
(a) Making artificial icebergs for zoos in the United States (b) Lifting water from the oceans (c) Welding iron in the Soviet Union (d) Traffic blocks in Holland

719. Lithopone is a mixture of zinc sulphide and barium sulphate. It is used as a paint. One of the reasons why it is a better paint than white lead, is that it:
(a) Is more bright (b) Is more white (c) Does not become black in air (d) Does not become yellow in air

720. Which of the following is not an organic source of energy?
(a) Coal (b) Wood (c) Natural gas (d) Uranium

721. During the mid ninteenth century, Daguerro-type portraits were very popular. A portrait image of a person was made on silver plated copper by developing the image with:
(a) 'Hypo' (sodium hypochlorite) solution
(b) Mercury vapour (c) Silver bromide
(d) An iodine solution

722. Paul Ehrlich is known as the 'father of chemotherapy'. Some of his contributions are mentioned here. Can you pick the false one?
(a) He studied the therapeutic effect of chemicals on the body (b) He discovered 'Sylvarsan', considered a wonder drug in 1920. (c) He studied the structure of protein (d) He studied the structure of chemicals and their effect on the body

723. More than 1,00,000 different dyes have been synthesized. The chemical part of the dye that absorbs light and produces colour is called a:
(a) Neon (b) Chromophore (c) Natural pigment (d) Photochrome

724. During industrial extraction of lead metal from its main ore galena, we are also able to recover as by-products, important quantities of:
(a) Gold (b) Silver (c) Chromium (d) Diamonds

725. Some latex paints are useful, giving best results for walls on the outside of buildings as they are not easily affected by light, nor are they rubbed off by rain or water and can be easily cleaned by water. Can you identify them from the following?
(a) Styrene-butadiene forms rubber latex emulsions (b) Polyvinyl acetate (c) Blends of linseed oil with latex emulsion containing styrene-butadiene (d) Acrylic latex paints

726. When limestone is heated in a lime-kiln we get:
(a) Quicklime and carbon dioxide (b) Slaked lime and carbon dioxide (c) Milk of lime (d) Calcium hydroxide and carbon dioxide

727. Some compounds turn dark when exposed to light. They are, therefore, used in photography. A metal used for making such compounds is:
(a) Chromium (b) Nickel (c) Aluminium (d) Silver

728. Clock pendulums must maintain exact time by swinging in a constant rhythm. The motion of the pendulum depends on its length, which is affected by temperature changes in the weather. Therefore, clock pendulums are made of 'invar', a special steel which is very little affected by temperature changes. Invar steel contains 36%:

(a) Cobalt (b) Aluminium (c) Copper (d) Nickel

729. There are various methods of combating desease. Use of chemical compounds for treatment of desease, is called:
(a) Chemical treatment (b) Chromatography (c) Chemotherapy (d) Pharmacology

730. Nitroglycerine is an uncontrollably explosive substance. Alfred Nobel of Sweden discovered that it could be absorbed in a porous dried clay called kieselguhr. This led to its commercial use as a controlled explosive. Alfred Nobel made a fortune out of this discovery from where he started the fund for awarding Nobel Prizes. What was the explosive that he discovered?
(a) Gun powder (b) Dynamite (c) T.N.T. (d) Napalm

731. Small quantities of substances contained in mixtures can be separated by means of absorption on paper or in a column of kieselguhr. This is a very effective method of isolating, separating and identifying small quantities of substances, known as:
(a) Colloidal chemistry (b) Chromatography (c) Viscometry (d) Polarography

732. Acetylene is mixed with oxygen and burned to produce:
(a) Acetaldehyde (b) Carbon ash for fertilizers (c) A hot flame for cutting steel

(d) Heat for the manufacture of nuclear-grade material

733. Toilet soaps contain an oil that has a lot of free fatty acids, chief among which is oleic acid. Can you identify this oil which is an important constituent of toilet soaps?
(a) Coconut oil (b) Margarine (c) Palm oil (d) Sunflower oil

734. Electric bulbs contain a metal filament. When the electric current is switched on, the filament gets heated and gives off a bright light that illuminates the room. In order to prevent the hot metal filament from getting burnt, the bulb is filled with:
(a) Methane (b) An inert gas (c) Chlorine (d) Carbon dioxide

735. Aluminium, deposited as vapour on glass, forms good mirrors, essentially because:
(a) It has better shine than silver (b) It does not scratch (c) The coating is much smoother (d) It does not tarnish in air

736. Victor Grignard was awarded the Nobel Prize for making useful compounds by joining organic compounds to:
(a) Inorganic iron (b) Magnesium and Iodine elements on the inorganic side (c) Proteins which, are complex biochemicals (d) Radioactive matter

737. Marble is the most decorative and highly-valued, natural stone for floors, tiles, pil-

lars and bathing rooms. It is snow-white, when pure. Coloured marble is formed due to the presence of some minerals which impart beautiful coloured lines, streaks and shades. Can you pick the false one?
(a) Iron oxide gives a red colour to marble (b) Ferrous silicates give green shade to marble (c) Zinc oxide may give a brown colour (d) Graphite may give red and black lines

738. Special strike-anywhere matches can light a fire by rubbing against any rough surface. They do not require a matchbox strip for rubbing. The matchheads contain an oxidizing agent, such as potassium chlorate and a sulphide of:
(a) Iron (b) Phosphorous (c) Carbon (d) Cobalt

739. Sulphur is one of the most basic elements known from early times. Some of its uses are mentioned here. Can you pick the false one?
(a) In making matches and fireworks (b) For making sulphuric acid (c) For making glass (d) For vulcanising rubber

740. Polymerized methyl methacrylate is a colourless, transparent plastic that becomes soft on heating. It is known by various trade names mentioned here. Can you pick the false one?

(a) Plexiglass (b) Lucite (c) Crystallite
(d) Freon

741. Robert Boyle published his great book, 'The Sceptical Chymist', in the seventeenth century. What was he not sceptical about? (a) The four elements of nature of the Greek thinkers (b) The three elements of nature of the alchemists (c) The old views on elements (d) The existence of unmixed elements

742. Earlier, gramophone records were made from a natural resin, shellac, which comes from insects on trees. Nowadays, records, lighter in weight, are made from synthetic plastics like:
(a) Polythene (b) PVC (or polyvinyl chloride) (c) Polyacrylonitrile (d) Bakelite

743. Which of the following salts of sodium is sometimes added to municipal water so that it helps in making teeth strong and prevents dental cavities?
(a) Chloride (b) Fluoride (c) Sulphate (d) Iodide

744. The linkage between two or more atoms is known as:
(a) A chain (b) A chemical knot (c) A bond (d) An atomic line

745. Kannada, in ancient India, put forward the idea that matter is made of small particles

that cannot be broken up or divided. He call them 'anu' (or atoms). In ancient Greece, a similar view was put forward by: (a) Archimedes (b) Empedocles (c) Aristotle (d) Ptolemy

746. When a hydrated chemical loses water of hydration attatched to its molecules, the phenomenon is called:
(a) Phosphorescence (b) Radiation (c) Efflorescence (d) Luminescence

747. Soap forms lather (foam) with difficulty when the water is:
(a) Soft (b) Hard (c) Chlorinated (d) Fresh

748. Substances like heavy water, which control the speed of neutrons that cause fast chain reactions in a nuclear reactor for making energy, are called:
(a) Speed-breakers (b) Chain-breakers (c) Moderators (d) Inert chemicals

749. On the average, every second or third object of modern civilisation that we come in contact with has something to do with sulphuric acid, a chemical involved in making pigments, fertilizers, explosives, batteries, fibres, detergents among other things. Every year the world consumption of sulphuric acid, in tonnes is:
(a) 90,000 (b) 2 million (c) 70 million (d) 200 million

750. Hydrogen peroxide has different uses. One of the special uses of hydrogen peroxide is in:
(a) Dyes (b) Creams (c) Plant nutrition (d) Rocket fuels

751. Karat is a measure of the fineness of gold. 24 Karats (or carats) is almost pure gold, that is, 99.99% pure. Any item marked as 'Gold' in the U.S.A.:
(a) Could be only 50% gold (b) Would be at least 18-carat gold (c) Should be 24-carat gold (d) Could be an alloy of gold, with gold being the dominant metal

752. The lanthanides and actinides are a group of closely-related elements which are often found in the products of nuclear fission of heavy elements. They can be separated from one another and from other nuclear products by:
(a) Evaporation on a metal foil (b) Ion-exchange chromatography (c) Distillation (d) Slow melting

753. A lilac-coloured flame is produced on heating:
(a) Sodium in a flame (b) Cobalt in a flame (c) Potassium in a flame (d) Methane in oxygen

754. When different quantities of electric current are passed through solutions of substances like salts and acids or through

molten matter, different quantities of chemical reactions take place. Whose name is associated with remarkable studies in this field?
(a) J. van't Hoff (b) Ernest Rutherford (c) Michael Faraday (d) Emil Fischer

755. Which of the following facts, most strongly suggests that life began in the seas and oceans?
(a) There is water in living creatures (b) Oxygen is breathed by human beings and animals (c) There is salt in the body (d) Most creatures have to drink water to survive

756. Which inert element is used in air balloons?
(a) Hot air (b) Hydrogen (c) Helium (d) Fluorine

757. Sodium dissolves in cold, liquid ammonia to produce a blue-coloured solution. The solution is a strong reducing agent. The blue colour and reducing property arises because:
(a) Sodium releases an electon (b) Ammonia dissociates (c) Sodium nitride is formed (d) Of reaction with dissolved oxygen

758. The most abundant element in the earth's crust is:
(a) Oxygen (b) Silicon (c) Hydrogen (d) Iron

759. In 1972, the tallest chimney in the world was 1,250 feet high. It was as tall as the Empire State Building. The purpose of this chimney was to release the smoke at a high level in the air to save the surrounding area from pollution by gases like sulphur dioxide released from a copper-making industrial plant. Can you identify where this chimney is located?
(a) Shanghai, China (b) Ontario, Canada
(c) Hamburg, Germany (d) Turin, Italy

760. The human blood is a complex mixture of biochemicals. It contains many proteins. These can be separated by moving them in a solution under the influence of:
(a) A magnetic force (b) An electric field
(c) Intense radiation (d) An organic solvent

761. Gold is found in nature as a lustrous, yellow metal in gold-bearing rocks. The leading places in the world where gold deposits are found are mentioned here. Can you pick the false one?
(a) South Africa (b) Brazil (c) Siberia
(d) Alaska

762. Neoprene is a polymer made by using acetylene as a raw material. It is used as:
(a) Plastic for dining tables (b) Plastic for car panels (c) Rubber in diving suits (d) Material for electrical switches

763. Which of the following ages cannot be determined by radioactive carbon dating?

(a) A long-living, thousand-year old Sequoia tree (b) Samples of rock from old mountains (c) Remains of an animal from an Inca temple in Mexico (d) An old piece of wood from an Egyptian tomb

764. The kinetic theory of matter helped a great deal in understanding the behaviour of gases. Which of the following statements did not belong to it?
(a) Gases are made up of small particles, called molecules (b) The molecules in a gas are always moving (c) When the gas is heated by raising its temperature, the molecules move faster (d) When molecules collide, they lose energy

765. Gun-shots are made of lead metal with a little arsenic. The arsenic is added to increase the:
(a) Power of fire (b) Range of fire (c) Brittleness of lead (d) Weight of fire

766. Madam Curie was awarded a Nobel Prize in Physics. She got a second Nobel Prize in Chemistry in 1911 for the discovery of:
(a) Acids in bitter fruit (b) Radium, a radioactive element (c) Calcium, a nutrient (d) The atom

767. Archaeologists were not sure whether farmers in ancient Egypt grew wheat before the reign of the great Pharaoh dynasty. When some wheat was found near

the river Nile, it was found to be 6,300 years old, that is, it was grown much before the time of the Pharaohs. How was this established?
(a) By measuring the depth at which wheat was found (b) By testing the wheat with very sensitive chemicals (c) By measuring the difference in colour when compared to modern wheat (d) By measuring radiation from radioactive carbon in the wheat

768. Food has to be stored and transported after it is picked from fields and orchards. A lot of money is spent by the food processing industry for preserving fruit and food stuffs. Which of the following is used in preserving fruit and foodstuffs?
(a) Nitrites (b) Nitric oxide (c) Oxygen (d) Sulphite solution

769. Sir Ernest Rutherford is well-known for his suggestion of a model of the atom. However, the Nobel Prize awarded to him in the year 1908, was for his studies on the chemistry of:
(a) Plastics (b) Radioactive matter (c) Explosives (d) Free radicals

770. The spectrum of a molecule is so detailed that a molecule can be identified by its spectrum:
(a) With great difficulty (b) Only by test-tube analysis (c) Only if it is small (d) Easily, like a fingerprint

771. Which of the following gases cannot be kept in a glass bottle because it chemically reacts with glass?
(a) Fluorine (b) Chlorine (c) Sulphur dioxide (d) Methane

772. Mercury is the shiny thread in a thermometer. It has been known since ancient times. It can dissolve many metals. But there are some metals which it cannot dissolve. These are mentioned here. Can you pick the false one?
(a) Iron (b) Cobalt (c) Nickel (d) Silver

773. The centre of the earth is a core, mainly containing:
(a) Iron that creates a magnetic field (b) Copper that gives radiation (c) Silicon that forms clay (d) Magnesium that colours volcanic flames

774. Hair, fingernails and hoofs are all made of:
(a) Fat (b) Iron (c) Vitamins (d) Proteins

775. Air containing too much of carbon dioxide is bad for health. In industry, however, carbon dioxide is a useful gas. Some of its uses are mentioned here. Can you pick the false one?
(a) Under pressure it is used as soda water (b) It can be cooled and used as a refrigerant (c) It is used in preserving fruit (d) It is used in fire-extinguishers

76. Temporary hardness in water can be removed by boiling it. This type of hardness is due to the presence of calcium or magnesium:
(a) Sulphates (b) Carbonates (c) Bicarbonates (d) Chlorides

777. The atoms in molecules are arranged in space at well-defined distances. This gives the molecule a definite shape. Which of the following is incorrect?
(a) Methane gas molecules have a tetrahedral shape (b) A square planar shape is found in nickel tetrachloride (c) Acetylene is round (d) Phosphorous pentoxide is like two pyramids joined at their apices

778. Some kinds of jewellery are cleaned by soap, water and a drop of ammonia. Which of the following should not be cleaned in this way?
(a) Silver-filled jewellery (b) Gold-filled jewellery (c) Rolled-gold plate jewellery (d) Gold-electroplated jewellery

779. An effective air-pollution control equipment is an attachment that electrically attracts pollutant particles in hot, escaping gases. It is known as:
(a) An air purifier (b) A gas condenser (c) An electric condenser (d) A electrostatic precipitator

780. Polythene (or polyethylene) is a tough wax-like polymer used in many ways, some of which are mentioned here. Can you pick the false one?
(a) Bread-wrappers (b) Plastic pipes
(c) Construction materials of plastic
(d) Candles

781. When Napoleon marched on Egypt, Berthollet went as a scientific adviser. He observed that salt and calcium carbonate (lime) were being formed and deposited on the lake shores by a chemical reaction. However, he found that the very large (excessive) quantity of salt on the lake caused this reaction to:
(a) Go faster (b) Slow down (c) Stop altogether (d) Reverse direction

782. Mercury has many uses. Some are mentioned here. Can you pick the false one?
(a) In thermometers (b) In mercury vapour lamps (c) In photographic paper (d) In metal amalgams for tooth filling

783. In the olden days, iron was extracted from its ore by crude heating methods. Where did some of the Eskimos in snow-covered lands get iron from?
(a) A meteorite that fell from the sky
(b) Iron metal found deep in the earth
(c) From volcanic eruptions (d) Rocks near mineral springs

784. The orange coloured part of the flame of a burning matchstick is as hot as 900 degrees centigrade. The sun is a burning ball of fire. The hottest flame on earth may not be as hot as the coldest part of the sun, that is its surface. The lowest temperature of the sun, at its surface is:
(a) 1000°C (b) 2000°C (c) 5000°C
(d) 10,000°C

785. Colour photography using a camera is a fascinating hobby as well as a profession. A colour photographic film, usually has three colour-sensitive layers. These are mentioned here. Can you pick the false one?
(a) On the top is a layer sensitive to blue light (with a filter that prevents blue light from going further down)(b) Next is a layer that is sensitive to green light (c) Next is a layer sensitive to red (d) Next is a layer sensitive to yellow light

786. Petroleum refineries remove chemical compounds that contain sulphur in order to:
(a) Increase the mileage of petrol (b) Make pure, white petrol (c) Prevent pollution of the air by sulphur (d) Use the sulphur to make other compounds cheaply

787. Some herbs and plants that were used in olden times for making drugs are used even today for making drugs. Can you pick the false one?

(a) Belladona (deadly nightshade)
(b) Foxglove (digitalis) (c) Marigold
(d) The plant of castor oil

788. Acetic acid has many applications. Can you pick the false one?
(a) In making acetone (b) In making dyes
(c) In making soap (d) In making waterproofing fabrics

789. When we talk about the quantity of reserves of copper, iron or any other metal, we mean the:
(a) Total amount of the metal present in the Earth's crust (b) The estimate of metal that could be extracted at any cost from known and estimated deposits (c) The known deposits as of now from which it could be extracted at reasonable cost (d) The quantity of metal that would remain after meeting domestic consumption

790. 'Accelerators', in rubber technology, are organic sulphur compounds used as:
(a) Fillers (b) Carbon black binders for tyres (c) Catalysts for vulcanisation (d) Speed increasers for nylon tyres

791. England was interested in using nitrogen for making fertilizers. In Germany, nitrogen was being explored for making explosives. When in Germany a scientist found how to make ammonia from

nitrogen and hydrogen, this discovery is said to have:
(a) Prolonged the Second World War
(b) Immediately benefited agriculture
(c) Prolonged the First World War
(d) Ended the Cold War

792. Before the advent of synthetic dyes, natural dyes were used. In ancient times, it is said that Alexander the Great deceived the Persians by pretending that his army was wounded. He splashed his soldiers with a red dye, which is thought to have been madder juice which contains the dye:
(a) Mauve (b) Alizarin (c) Fluorescein
(d) Phenolphthalein

793. Which of the following is matter that contains only two chemical elements?
(a) Tea (b) Water (c) Coffee (d) Sugar

794. Acetylene is the starting point for making many synthetic materials, some of which are mentioned here. Can you pick the false one?
(a) Plastics like PVC (b) Textile yarn
(c) Glucose (d) Drugs

795. A laboratory or industrial process of manufacture or extraction of a chemical often involves many steps or stages. When a series of chemical reactions are involved the yield of final product obtained from the starting raw material is likely to:

(a) Remain constant (b) Increase
(c) Decrease (d) Be less than one percent

796. Sodium nitrite is a pale-yellow, crystalline solid that combines with aniline to form diazonium salts from which we get:
(a) Hydrazine (b) Azo-dyes (c) Ink (d) Paints

797. Pure silver metal is very soft. For making jewellery or cutlery like table knives and spoons, it is hardened by alloying with a small amount of:
(a) Iron or aluminium (b) Tin or zinc (c) Copper or nickel (d) Platinum or gold

798. Around room temperature, we use a mercury thermometer. Far below that, around minus 272°C, we use a helium vapour-pressure thermometer. Even further below, in order to measure temperature, we have to use:
(a) A special mercury thermometer (b) Magnetic properties (c) Sound waves (d) Atomic clocks

799. Nuclear energy from atoms can be used in making powerful and dangerous weapons. A powerful, 24-megaton bomb was accidentally dropped in 1961, but one of the safety devices prevented it from exploding. The bomb had far more explosive force

than the entire Second World War or the Vietnam War. Where did this happen?
(a) In Greenland (b) In Wales (c) In North Carolina (U.S.A.) (d) In Kamchatka (U.S.S.R.)

800. In order to prevent the decay of teeth, which of the following is contained in some toothpastes?
(a) Stannous fluoride (b) Tin chloride (c) Sodium fluoride (d) Iron sulphate

Section 9

801. Industrial gases can be purified to some extent before releasing them, for preventing air pollution. Some methods are mentioned here, by which the quantity of contaminant particles present can be reduced. Can you pick the false one?
(a) Ultrasonic vibration (b) Passing ultraviolet radiation (c) Centrifugal separation (d) Spraying fine jets of water

802. The normal pressure of the air that surrounds us at mean sea level is about one atmosphere. The pressure of matter at the centre of the earth is 1.2 million atmospheres. At the centre of the sun it may be:
(a) 2 million atmospheres (b) 10 million atmospheres (c) 1 billion atmospheres (d) 10 billion atmospheres

803. Louis Pasteur picked up crystals of sodium ammonium tartarate by tweezers and then physically separated them into two natural types of crystals, each of which:
(a) Was one half of a whole (b) Was a mirror image of the other (c) Possessed an opposite electrical charge (d) Possessed an opposite colour

804. An oil slick is a thin film of petroleum that spreads for miles on the high seas, caused by the spillage of oil from large tankers. Efforts are made to removed it by different methods mentioned here. Can you pick the irrelevant one?
(a) Physical removal by special vessels (b) Chemical means (c) Biochemical degradation (d) Radiation

805. From which source-chemical you can get acetic acid, petrol additives and ethylene di-bromide?
(a) Bromine (b) Ethylene (c) Methane (d) Alcohol

806. It is always safe to take precautions while handling chemicals by wearing goggles, masks, gloves and aprons. When you want to mix sulphuric acid and water one should take the precaution of:
(a) Adding water to the acid (b) Adding acid to the water (c) Adding whichever is lighter to the heavier one (d) Avoiding sunlight

807. Benzo-alpha-pyrene (BAP), a cancer causing pollutant is released by the burning of coal. It is ten times more in an urban area than in a rural area. In some areas the effect of this air pollutant on people who do not smoke cigarettes may go upto:
(a) An equivalent effect of one-tenth of those who smoke (b) An effect less than that of those who smoke (c) An effect equal to that of those who smoke two packets of cigarettes without filters (d) An effect equal to that of those who smoke two cigarettes a day

808. Mercury is a toxic substance that is produced in many industries and contaminates the environment. Which country was the first to establish a standard (limit) upto which mercury could be allowed to be tolerated in industrial effluents (waste)?
(a) U.S.A. (b) Germany (c) Russia (d) Japan

809. Glyptal (alkyd resins) are polyesters of acids and polyhydric alcohols. They are used in the manufacture of:
(a) Rubber and tyres (b) Paints and lacquers (c) Printing inks (d) Nail polish

810. Which of the following does not contain carbohydrates?
(a) Wheat flour (b) Cellulose (c) Wax (d) Starch

811. When stars explode, new stars may form out of the collection of condensed matter from various stars. This would already contain carbon and iron. Using carbon as a catalyst, there would be a steady supply of neutrons to form elements heavier than iron, such as bismuth. Such a star is known as:
(a) An heavy metal maker (b) An explosion cloud (c) An inter-stellar·gas (d) A second generation star

812. When a mixture of iron oxide and aluminium powder, known as thermite, is heated, intense heat is generated. This fact is made use of in:
(a) Making iron (b) Welding steel
(c) Soldering (d) Cutting of metals

813. Children love to play with balloons. These are often filled with hydrogen gas, which is lighter than air. Which of the following is used as a source of hydrogen for filling of balloons that is convenient and can be carried around?
(a) Calcium metal (b) Sodium borohydride
(c) Lithium hydride (d) Sodium formate

814. Barium is a metal whose compounds are used in many ways, some of which are mentioned here. Can you pick the false one?

(a) In paper-making industry (b) For taking X-rays of the stomach (c) In medicine (d) In food preservation

815. High techniques are involved in purifying water for drinking purposes by removing as many contaminants as possible. Organic, bad-smell causing compounds and even carcinogens (cancer-causing substances) are removed from drinking water by:
(a) Heating at 50°C (b) Settling in tanks (c) Filtering through pellets of carbon (d) Aeration in an oxygen-rich environment

816. How much iron can a typical blast furnace produce in one day?
(a) 50 to 100 million tonnes (b) One million tonnes (c) 50,000 to 1,00,000 tonnes (d) 3000 to 6000 tonnes

817. The positively charged particles in the nucleus of an atom repel each other, yet the nucleus remains intact. When a nucleus disintegrates, this energy is released. It is called the:
(a) Binding energy (b) Atomic energy (c) Calories (d) Electrostatic energy

818. Ethylene, which is obtained from crude petroleum, is a source-chemical for many things mentioned here. Can you pick the false one?

(a) Antifreeze for motor vehicles (b) Detergents (c) Printing inks (d) Polyvinyl chloride

819. Aluminium metal and its alloys can be used in various ways as containers. Some are mentioned here. Can you pick the false one?
(a) In cans for transporting milk (b) In pressure cookers (c) For canning dry foods (d) For canning foods preserved in an alkaline solution

820. Atomic nuclear reactors use heavy water. This is different from ordinary water only to the extent that in place of hydrogen it contains:
(a) Tritium, an heavier isotope of hydrogen
(b) Nitrogen, which is also a light element
(c) Deuterium, an heavier isotope of hydrogen (d) A radioactive element

821. Cinnabar, the most important ore of mercury is a reddish-brown sulphide with lustre existing in thin, transparent layers. It is found in the places mentioned here. Can you pick the false one?
(a) Spain (b) U.S.A. (c) England (d) China

822. In the freezer in your refrigerator at home, you have ice at a temperature of 0°C. In a deep freeze it may be -5°C. In the coldest part of the world it may be -42°C. At a

pressure of 20,000 atmospheres, we can have ice at:
(a) Only at ⁻50°C (b) Only at ⁻100°C (c) ⁻200°C (d) At 100°C, the temperature of steam

823. A piece of pumice stone is used for scrubbing dirt from hands and feet. Pumice is a colloidal solution of a:
(a) Solid in a solid (b) Solid in a liquid (c) Liquid in a solid (d) Gas in a solid

824. Biodegradable materials are those which:
(a) Spoil the biological environment (b) Are toxic (c) Can be broken down by bacteria (d) Are used for converting waste or garbage into greenery

825. Sodium is highly reactive and can cause fire and explosion with water. Therfore, on a commercial scale, it is prepared as:
(a) An oxide (b) An amalgam of mercury (c) An alloy of lead (d) A tin-plated metal

826. Crystallographers of the ninteenth century measured angles of crystals and their various geometric qualities. It gradually became clear that the beautiful forms of crystals come from the packing of elementary matter in:
(a) Different lattice blocks (b) The same lattice arrangement (c) Various atoms (d) Various shapes

827. Which of the following is used as a thickener in paints and lipstick?
(a) Calcium carbonate (b) Bentonite
(c) Soap (d) Ethyl chloride

828. Water collects on roofs and floors of caves and deposits calcium bicarbonate, which decomposes to calcium carbonate. Tall, white, regular pillars are formed when columns of calcium carbonate grow down from the roof and others move up from the floor. These fascinating works of nature are called:
(a) Spirals (b) Chromite and cobaltite
(c) Stalagmites and stalactites (c) Calcite and feldspar

829. Constantan is an industrial alloy consisting of 60% copper and 40% nickel. It is an example of a:
(a) Solid-solid reaction (b) Solid solution
(c) Catalyst (d) Chemical reaction

830. Acids combine with bases to form:
(a) Water and heat (b) Salt and water
(c) Colour and gas (d) Steam and crystals

831. It has been estimated by archaeologists, historians and scientists that the extraction of iron from crude ores was an art that was learnt by man as early as:
(a) 2,000 years ago (b) 3,000 years ago
(c) 4,000 years ago (d) 10,000 years ago

832. From wood we obtain cellulose. When this is reacted with carbon disulphide, we get Cellulose xanthate. On passing through fine holes (spinneretes) into acid we get:
(a) Enamel paint (b) Viscose fibre (c) A yellow azoic dye (d) An high explosive

833. Artificial rubies and sapphires can be made by heating alumina in:
(a) Burning methane (b) An oxy-acetylene flame (c) An oxy-hydrogen flame (d) An electric furnace

834. On Mondays, Wednesdays and Fridays it is a particle. On Tuesdays, Thursdays and Saturdays it is a wave. On Sundays it takes rest. This is a comic description of one of nature's most dynamic and elusive particles. Can you identify it?
(a) The silicon chip (b) The atomic nucleus (c) The electron (d) The alpha particle

835. Lavoisier, the famous scientist of France discovered that mercury combines with oxygen to form mercuric oxide, an orange powder. When this is heated, it gives back the same quantity of mercury and oxygen. This led him to the conclusion that a chemical reaction does not change:
(a) Matter (b) Mercury (c) The total quantity of matter (d) The total quantity of oxygen

836. Zeolites are alumino - silicates. They can absorb particles upto a certain size and thus behave as sieves for filtering:
(a) Atoms (b) Molecules (c) Colloids (d) Carbon soot in polluted air

837. The horror of a surgical operation was great in the days when there was no proper anaesthetic. Patients being taken for operation, yelled and cried. This nightmare ended when ether was replaced in the mid-ninteenth century by:
(a) Nitrous oxide (b) Acetone (c) Chloroform (d) Ammonia

838. Moving metal parts of machinery need lubrication in order to reduce friction and heat. Lubrication products were derived from petroleum and coal, in 1848, by:
(a) James Young (b) James Watt (c) George Stephenson (d) Edward Jenning

839. In atactic propylene, the groups attatched to the main-line polymer chain are not aligned to each other in any regular pattern. Therefore, we get tough polymers having very little elasticity that are useful in making the following articles. Can you pick the false one?
(a) Car-battery cases (b) Steering wheels of cars (c) Electric torch bodies (d) Washing machine agitators

840. You may not have heard of a cold flame because flames are very hot. A cold, green flame can be made by passing carbon dioxide over warm:

(a) Bronze (b) White phosphorous (c) Grey tin (d) Green candles

841. Vanishing creams are applied to the skin to give a smooth, thin covering. They do not vanish. They consist of a suspension of:

(a) Clay in oil (b) Stearic acid in water (c) Protein in grease (d) Alum in wax

842. The lightest gas on earth is:

(a) Helium (b) Oxygen (c) Hydrogen (d) Chlorine

843. Amorphous minerals possess an atomic structure in which the geometric arrangement is:

(a) Very regular (b) Varies (c) Well-defined (d) Unknown

844. If white light is passed through a colloidal solution containing fine suspended particles of gold, then the scattered light seen in a direction different from that of the incident light is coloured:

(a) Red (b) Blue (c) Green (d) Yellow

845. Pure silicon is used in the:

(a) Electronics industry (b) Textile industry (c) Paint industry (d) Pharmaceutical industry

846. Hard water can be softened in:
(a) A calorimeter (b) An ion exchanger
(c) A chromatograph (d) An earthenware
pot

847. Treatment of cotton waste with acetic acid
results in the manufacture of cellulose
acetate, which is used in:
(a) Cigarette filters (b) Plastic ash trays
(c) Foam rubber (d) Azo-dyes

848. The third planet that revolves round the
sun is the earth on which we live. On the
earth we find elements like iron, magnesium, silicon, oxygen, carbon, hydrogen
and helium. The other planets, which are
also nearer to the sun, namely Mars, Venus
and Mercury, have:
(a) A different composition (b) A similar
composition (c) Totally different elements
(d) Elements opposite to those found on
earth

849. An ounce of gold can be beaten with
hammers into a sheet of thin foil that can
cover:
(a) One page of a small book (b) A six feet
by three feet dining table top (c) The floor
of a room ten feet by ten feet (d) A road
ten feet wide and hundred feet long

850. The secret of the highly explosive power
of explosives like TNT is that:

(a) They burn rapidly in air (b) They create destructive shock waves (c) They contain oxygen in the chemical itself (d) The chemical releases oxygen like a bullet in the air

851. Red phosphorous is used in making:
(a) Safety match-striking surfaces (b) Red dyes for plastics (c) Red plastics (d) Air fresheners

852. Alcohol for industry is being made from a variety of plant sources. Which of the following is not relevant as a source of ethyl alcohol?
(a) Beetroot (b) Potatoes (c) Cane sugar (d) Peas

853. The atomic weight of lead contained in a sample of thorite ore from Ceylon was found to be 207.77. Richards at Harvard found that the atomic weight of lead in a sample of ore from Norway was different, namely, 206.08. This led to the discovery of:
(a) Isomers in nature (b) The metal thorium (c) Occurrence of isotopes (d) Radium, a radioactive element

854. When alpha-particles (carrying positive charges) were directed towards a sheet of thin gold foil, most of them passed through, but some were thrown back. This

result led to the conclusions mentioned here. Can you pick the false one?
(a) The atom consists mostly of empty space (b) The centre of the atom has a positive charge (c) The atom has a heavy centre (d) The centre of the atom is rotating

855. Which of the following is not an anaesthetic?
(a) Ether (b) Trichloro-ethylene (c) Thiobarbiturates (d) Propane

856. The four bases, adenine, thymine, cytosine and guanine can be arranged in a variety of combinations like playing cards. The pattern of chains formed by these bases is the foundation for:
(a) The Krebs cycle (b) The genetic code, which determines height, colour of eyes and other characterstics (c) The photosynthetic role played by chlorophyll in green plants (d) Ten fingers on hands and feet

857. If ten birds pecked on the keys of a typewriter for millions of years, they could produce all the plays of Shakespeare. This creative vision suggests how life began on earth. What is the idea?
(a) Flying pieces from comets became birds (b) Gases dissolved in oceans became fishes (c) The high probability of a biochemical reaction over a long period of time (d) That ten atoms of carbon suddenly formed a chain of organic matter

858. Cosmetic powders and zinc ointments contain:
(a) Lead (b) Zinc carbonate (c) Zinc oxide (d) Zinc sulphate

859. Light coming from the sun is stored as energy in plants by the process of photosynthesis. This happens by converting carbon dioxide and water into:
(a) Chlorophyll (b) Carbohydrates (c) Green leaves (d) Plant hormones

860. Adding acids to cellulose gives gun-cotton from which we can make cordite. Cordite is:
(a) A rocket propellant (b) A bullet propellant (c) An insect repellant (d) An insulator

861. Nowdays we have motor-cycle helmets, small boats and many articles made of fibreglass embedded in resin, possessing high tensile strength and resistance to corrosion. Fibre-glass is a trade-name for fibres made of:
(a) Cotton (b) Plastic (c) Wool (d) Glass

862. The refrigerator cools your food and drink. The cooling is due to:
(a) The work of the electric motor (b) The expansion of the refrigerant gas (c) Expansion of ice (d) Reaction of the refrigerant gas

863. The gases ethylene and acetylene (used in torches for welding steel) have been found on the planets:

(a) Mercury and Pluto (b) Mars and Venus (c) Jupiter and Saturn (d) Neptune and Uranus

864. A lot of effort is being made to try and preserve food articles. Which of the following is used as a preservative for food? (a) Alum (b) Sodium benzoate (c) Salicylic acid (d) Ferric chloride

865. While there is no atmosphere on the moon, the earth has air which we breathe. It extends for many hundred miles up in the sky and supports life upto a height of 4 miles above the mean sea level. Air is a mixture of gases, mostly, nitrogen, oxygen, water vapour, carbon dioxide, rare gases and pollutants. What is the approximate weight of all this air? (a) 1 million tons (b) 4000 billion tons (c) 5500 trillion tons (d) 8600 quadrillion tons

866. There are huge spots on the sun, bigger than the size of the earth. Flares that are thirty times taller than the earth, explode and the sun shoots out into space many things mentioned here. Can you pick the false one? (a) X-rays (b) Radio waves (c) Electrically charged particles (d) Radioactive carbon

867. When atoms join together to form chemical bonds without transferring any electrons

but rather, by sharing them, they are said to be united by a covalent bond. Which of the following does not have a chemical bond that is covalent?

(a) Acetylene (b) Oxygen (c) Copper sulphide (d) Wax from petroleum

868. We get many benefits from appliances and machines that use electricity, which is a flow of electrons. 'Electron' means 'amber' and 'Electra' was the daughter of Agamemnon in Greek mythology. 'Electra' means:

(a) The fastest (b) The bright one (c) The beautiful (d) The wise one

869. Hypnotism is a powerful art of suggestion. Under the influence of hypnotism, subjects may report as normal, a slight smell from:

(a) An oxygen cylinder (b) An ammonia bottle (c) A source of pure hydrogen gas (d) A source of pure nitrogen gas

870. For charging sub-atomic particles to high-speeds and energies, a big device is used that may be upto two miles long. It is known as a:

(a) Wilson cloud chamber (b) Linear accelerator (c) Cathode-ray tube (d) Fast-breeder reactor

871. When man landed on the moon in 1969, he stepped on its surface wearing shoes

whose soles were made of silicone rubber because it:
(a) Is very hard and enables stepping on moon-craters (b) Can withstand extreme temperatures (c) Is a good reflector of light (d) The softest rubber made so far

872. Tobacco is kept moist by adding:
(a) Sugars like glucose (b) Polyhydric alcohols (c) A drop of vegetable oil (d) Gums

873. Calcium carbonate occurs widely in nature in a variety of forms. Which of the following is not a form of calcium carbonate?
(a) Chalk (b) Granite (c) Marble (d) Limestone

874. Sometimes moulds (fungus) grow on bread or grains, like rice, corn and beans. These moulds (fungus) produce a carcinogenic (cancer-causing) poison, namely:
(a) Sodium phosphate (b) Triglyceride (c) Aflatoxin (d) Alfalfa

875. Sometimes two liquids do not dissolve but get finely scattered in each other, forming what is known as a colloidal solution. Which of the following is not a colloidal solution of a liquid in another liquid?
(a) Latex from the rubber tree (b) Photographic emulsions (c) Soap in water (d) Homogenized milk

876. Modern drugs are being prepared to tailor-cut requirements of medical problems by suitable designing of chemical structures. Some basic qualities in a drug, that are desrable, are mentioned here. Can you pick the false one?
(a) It can cure (b) It has the least amount of side-effects (c) It is easy to make (d) It is not bitter in taste

877. Substances that do not vapourise easily are called non-volatile substances. When these are dissolved in a liquid like benzene, it:
(a) Boils at a higher temperature (b) Boils at a lower temperature (c) Freezes (d) Increases in volume

878. Joseph Lister discovered 'carbolic acid' for use in antiseptic surgery in 1834 which saved many mothers during childbirth in those days. 'Carbolic acid' was the name used for:
(a) Opium (b) Phenol (c) Nutmeg (d) Chloroform

879. Carl Wilhelm Scheele was a famous Swedish scientist. He discovered a number of gases which are mentioned here. Can you pick the false one?
(a) Oxygen (b) Chlorine (c) Silicon fluoride (d) Bromine

880. When atoms like those of chlorine or oxygen pick up an electron, they release

energy and assume a more stable form. This energy released is said to be a measure of the:
(a) Explosive power of the atom (b) Electron affinity (c) Electrochemical potential (d) Nuclear stability

881. Hydrogen peroxide is used as:
(a) An enamel solvent (b) A solvent for paint (c) An antiseptic in toothpaste (d) A refrigerant

882. Grease is applied to parts of a motor vehicle for smooth movement. Greases are, essentially, lubrication oils made into a jelly by:
(a) Adding wax (b) Blowing air under presure (c) Soaps of fatty acids (d) Churning of starch

883. The brownish-white deposit on kettles, heating elements and utensils formed by boiling water is due to:
(a) Permanent hardness of water (b) Temporary hardness of water (c) Moisture in the air (d) Reaction of sulphur dioxide in the air with hot water

884. Soil is a natural medium for growth of land plants. Organic soil contains organic matter upto a depth of:
(a) Six inches (b) One foot (c) Two and-a-half feet (d) Ten feet

885. Cellophane is used as a plastic wrapper. It is made from:
(a) Cellulose (b) Phenol (c) Gum (d) Petroleum

886. Metal objects, like sheets of steel, gather a coating of rust if exposed to the air. Before galvanizing or electroplating, the metal has to be cleaned by dipping in a bath of dilute sulphuric acid. This is known as:
(a) De-rusting (b) Pickling (c) Acidification (d) Annealing

887. Excess of phosphate and nitrate ions from fertilizers can contaminate water in ponds and lakes by encouraging excessive:
(a) Release of heat (b) Increase in salt (c) Growth of algae, a species of water plant (d) Increase of oxygen

888. Graphite is a good conductor of electricity, and is difficult to melt because it possesses a special chemical structure. It has a variety of uses mentioned here. Can you pick the false one?
(a) In making heat-resistant crucibles for casting metals (b) In making slates for writing with chalk (c) For dynamo 'brushes' (d) For making heat-resistant paints

889. Water requires to be heated before it boils and becomes steam. The energy supplied by the heat is used in breaking hydrogen bonds between:

(a) One molecule of water and another (b) The hydrogen and oxygen within a water molecule (c) Hydrogen atoms of two different water molecules (d) Water and the container

890. If you put a waterproof, nine-volt battery in a mug of water containing two teaspoonfuls of salt, the water will be broken into gases and bubbles will start forming. What are these gases?
(a) Fluorine and chlorine (b) Hydrogen and oxygen (c) Carbon dioxide and nitrogen (d) Sulphur dioxide and 'laughing gas'

891. A filler is a substance added to make a material less expensive, or for:
(a) Reducing its chemical activity (b) Changing its physical properties (c) Changing its acidity (d) Increasing its anti-rusting power

892. When vegetable matter decays at the bottom of lakes and ponds where there is limited air, it gives rise to 'marsh gas', which is:
(a) Butane (b) Chlorine (c) Oxygen (d) Methane

893. The pressure of air in a motor tyre is due to:
(a) Air particles hitting the tyre from inside (b) The solid state of compressed air

213

(c) Sticking of air particles on the tyre

(d) Displacement of vacuum from the tyre

894. Which Nobel Prize winner demonstrated that giant molecules exist in nature and also prepared some of them?
(a) Henri Becquerel (b) Hermann Staudinger (c) Berzelius (d) J. van't Hoff

895. The most widely used storage battery in cars, vehicles and domestic emergency lights is the:
(a) Leclanche cell (b) Lead accumulator (c) Cadmium cell (d) Alkaline battery

896. Destructive distillation of coal leads to a wide range of chemical products. Can you pick the false one?
(a) Paints and inks (b) Mauveine and other dyes (c) Bleaching agents (d) Synthetic fibres and plastics

897. Different forms of an element are called allotropes. Phosphorous occurs in three forms, each having its own colour. Can you pick the false one?
(a) Red phosphorous (b) White phosphorous (c) Green phosphorous (d) Black phosphorous

898. Excellent electrical and thermal insulators have been developed and used on a wide scale. These insulators use as bases for ceramic materials, almost pure:

(a) Clay and sand (b) Alumina and zirconia
(c) Glass and china clay (d) Ferrites

899. The earth and all forms of life on earth
are made of about a hundred chemical
elements of matter. These elements of
matter originally came many years ago,
from a star like our sun, or from:
(a) A 'white dwarf' star (b) A 'black hole'
in which objects vanish (c) A 'red giant'
star that makes carbon (d) A 'pulsar' object
that emits light at precise, regular intervals

900. When a photographic film is washed in
hypo (sodium thiosulphate) solution, the
chemical that has not reacted on exposure
to light is dissolved away and we get a
negative film whose dark areas are those
places that have been more exposed to
light. This process is known as:
(a) Developing the film (b) Fixing the film
(c) Washing the film (d) Sensitizing paper

Section 10

901. When pressure is slowly applied on a gas
that is capable of dissolving in a liquid,
then:
(a) More gas will dissolve in that liquid
(b)Less gas will dissolve (c) It will have no
effect (d) It will catch fire

902. When Napoleon the Great was defeated,
he complained of being slowly poisoned by

his captors. A few years back, scientists tested his hair and found that it contained arsenic oxide, a slow poison. This could have been added to his food, or may be due to the fact that hair powders used to contain arsenic oxide. How was arsenic oxide detected in a tiny piece of hair?
(a) By reaction with chemicals (b) By the difference in hair colour (c) By radioactive methods of detection (d) By measuring the curling of hair

903. Quartz, the mineral used in watches, is made of silicon and oxygen atoms joined in a network arrangement that is similar to:
(a) Graphite used in pencils (b) Iron metal (c) Diamond (d) The oxygen in the air

904. Iodine is used as sodium iodide in 'Iodised salt' for preventing the desease, goitre. Iodine is obtained from:
(a) Air (b) Dry wood (c) Sea weeds (d) Igneous rocks

905. The chemical elements, caesium and rubidium, both of which are metals, were discovered by splitting:
(a) The atom in a cyclotron (b) Light in a spectroscope (c) Hard ores in a furnace (d) Salt solution by an electric current

906. Stars are massive objects located at great distances in the sky. Some stars collapse

and shrink to a small size, known as white dwarfs. One barrel or drum of matter from such a star may be:
(a) Lighter than the air on earth (b) As heavy as iron on the moon (c) Heavier than lead on Mars (d) As heavy as a ship on earth

907. In olden times, acids and bases were known by their bitter taste and drastic chemical action that destroyed ordinary articles and even dissolved hard substances like metals. Today, an acid or a base is seen as a substance that can accept or give:
(a) A proton (b) A pair of electrons (c) A neutron (d) Water or air

908. Proteins are polymers (long chains) of amino acids. Which of the following polymers is not a protein?
(a) Hair (b) Wool (c) Finger-nails (d) DNA (genetic material)

909. Limestone is chemically attacked and eroded in cities by:
(a) Lead additives in petrol (b) Acetylene (c) Sulphurous gases (d) Carbon dioxide

910. Nowadays, R.C.C. (reinforced cement concrete) is used in roofs and pillars as a construction material of great strength. Concrete is a mixture of cement with sand. Microscopic examination has shown that the strength and hardness of R.C.C. is due to:

(a) The stickiness of clay in cement (b) Long, thread-like crystals (c) A metal bond (d) Long chains of carbon atoms

911. If pollen grains are suspended in water, they move about even when the water is undisturbed. This shows that:
(a) The gravitational pull of the earth is acting (b) Pollen is the lightest material on the planet earth (c) Molecules of water are moving continuously (d) A slow, chemical reaction is taking place

912. The black, striking head on the wooden splint of an ordinary match stick contains the following chemicals. Can you pick the false one?
(a) Sulphur (b) Magnesium (c) Antimony sulphide (d) Potassium chlorate

913. Sulphur is required in plants, as a nutrient element for:
(a) Making vitamins (b) Absorption of water (c) Making hormones (d) Absorption of fat

914. The glass that is commonly used for drinking water, or the glass used in window panes is 'soda glass', which contains oxides of three metals, namely, sodium, calcium and silicon. By replacing these metals we get different glasses mentioned here. Can you pick the false one?

(a) Sodium is replaced by potassium to give a higher melting glass (Jena glass) (b) Silicon by phosphorous (crown glass) (c) Calcium by lead to give a glass that refracts more light (flint glass) (d) Sodium and silicon are replaced by potassium and phosphorous, respectively, to give a higher refracting glass

915. Without a developer, the images created on photographic film would not be visible. When a photographic film is developed, there is a visible blackening of the film around the tiny particles where light has fallen. This developer is, chemically:
(a) A reducing agent (b) An oxidising agent (c) A catalyst (d) A solvent

916. Which of the following elements is a solid that is extracted as a liquid from the earth by boring a hole in the ground and pumping it out with super-heated steam?
(a) Copper (b) Sulphur (c) Lead (d) Iron

917. When ethylene is mixed with butadiene and made into long chains by polymerization, we get:
(a) Terylene (b) Hard plastic (c) Synthetic rubber (d) Synthetic sponge

918. In 1953, Stanley Miller passed a high voltage electric spark through a mixture of methane, water, ammonia and hydrogen. Glycine, an amino acid, was formed. This

experiment showed that, millions of years ago:
(a) Proteins could have been formed in the sky (b) Life on earth may have been started by a spark of lightning (c) Living creatures were made of glycine (d) Biochemical reactions used to take place at a high voltage

919. When cellulose from wood or cotton is cooked in large tanks containing caustic soda and then passed through a narrow slit into another tank containing acid, we get:
(a) Bakelite, an insulator (b) Rayon, a textile fibre (c) Cellophane, a paper-like plastic sheet (d) Unvulcanised rubber

920. Sodium tripolyphosphate is added to detergents to make them more effective. It acts by catching and removing metal ions present in water that cause hardness in it. Such chemical additives are known as:
(a) Lyophiles (b) Laundry soaps (c) Surfactants (d) Detergent builders

921. Sodium is sealed into parts of aircraft engine valves in order to:
(a) Protect them from corrosion (b) Make the valves open faster (c) Slow down the escape of exhaust gases (d) Quickly remove unwanted heat

922. In the hot temperatures of the sun and stars, violent nuclear reactions take place

to form heavy elements like lead and uranium. The abundance of heavy elements on earth suggests that our universe could be:

(a) A million years old (b) One billion years old (c) Ten billion years old (d) Hundred trillion years old

923. Vermilion is a red powder used in India in religious ceremonies, festivals and as an adornment by married women as a line on the hair-parting on the head. It is also used by artists. Chemically, vermilion is:

(a) Iron oxide (b) Mercuric sulphide (c) Platinum (d) Gold chloride

924. In modern surgery, metal pins are used for holding together broken bones. The pin that remains uncorroded in the body throughout the life of the patient is made of:

(a) Aluminium (b) Copper (c) Titanium (d) Lithium

925. Every day human beings, animals and plants are subjected to showers of hundreds of tiny particles passing through their body. These particles are formed in the earth's atmosphere by:

(a) The solar wind (b) Ozone from the upper layers of the air (c) Cosmic radiation from outer space (d) Electric sparks of lightning

926. An acid and an alcohol chemically combine to form important substances called:
(a) Ketones (b) Hydrocarbons (c) Esters (d) Hormones

927. Silt is finely divided, solid matter suspended in water. When silt from a river meets the sea at its mouth, it gets settled because the particles of silt carry electrostatic charges which are:
(a) Attracted by the ocean water (b) Neutralised by the salt of sea water (c) Built up by sea water (d) Increased when the movement of the river is stopped

928. When different colours in paint separate on drying and form patches and streaks, the phenomenon is known as flooding of the paint. It can be prevented by adding:
(a) Caustic soda (b) Lime (c) Stearic acid (d) Common salt

929. Oxidising agents are substances that can take up electrons or give atoms like oxygen and chlorine. Some oxidizing agents are mentioned here. Can you pick the false one?
(a) Potassium chlorate (b) Oxygen of the air (c) Glucose (d) Potassium dichromate

930. Acetone is the sweet-smelling solvent used in:
(a) Face-creams (b) Vanilla (c) Nail-polishes (d) Sweet-smelling erasers

931. "It would be a lovely thing to pass through life, together, hypnotized in our dreams: your dream for your country, our dream for science. Together we can serve humanity." So he married her and, both, husband and wife, were awarded the Nobel Prize in 1904. Who were this genius pair?
(a) The Einsteins (b) The Robinsons (c) The Svedbergs (d) The Curies

932. Enzymes, which catalyze biochemical reactions are very complex. They help in the reaction of very specific substances. This suggests that the enzyme and the reacting biochemicals are complementary to one another like a:
(a) Lock and key (b) Horse and a rider (c) Dog in his kennel (d) Leaf and a bud

933. Gypsum (calcium sulphate bihydrate) is added to cement in order to:
(a) Make it set (b) Retard the setting (c) Prevent it from decay (d) Make it fireproof

934. Large deposits of borax, an useful mineral, are found in:
(a) U.S.A. (b) U.S.S.R. (c) China (d) Spain

935. When molten glass is floated on a molten metal surface and then allowed to cool, we get a perfectly smooth glass finish, that needs no grinding or polishing after that. Can you name the metal?

(a) Iron (b) Silver (c) Tin (d) Copper

936. Which of the following metals has been used for building boats because it has resistance to corrosion by sea water?
(a) Tungsten (b) Nickel (c) Copper (d) Titanium

937. Glycerol belongs to the chemical family of alcohols. It is used for making things mentioned here. Can you pick the false one?
(a) In resins and varnishes having a glossy finish (b) Cosmetics (c) Matches (d) Explosives

938. Cement is used for making concrete, the chemical structure of which contains bonds between silicon and oxygen atoms. Although concrete is highly resistant to compression, it cannot withstand tension. If concrete is to be used in a place where it is to be subjected to tension, as in a bridge or a dome, then, it must be:
(a) Curved only upto 45 degrees (b) Dampened with water for eight days (c) Reinforced with steel (d) Made at least one foot thick

939. Sodium hydroxide is a basic raw material used in large quantities in the manufacture of items mentioned here. Can you pick the false one?

(a) Soap (b) Synthetic petrol (c) Synthetic fibre and dyes (d) Paper

940. The soot of candles, lanterns and chimneys is called carbon black. Carbon black (also known as lamp black) is made on a commercial scale by burning petroleum which is a hydrocarbon, in a limited supply of air. Its main uses are mentioned here. Can you pick the false one?
(a) As a filler for rubber in tyres (b) In printing ink (c) In the extraction of copper (d) In black pigments

941. Who was the first person to make a colour photograph?
(a) James Clerk Maxwell (b) William Harvey (c) Sir Humphrey Davy (d) Michael Faraday.

942. Which of the following acids is commonly used in batteries for cars?
(a) Hydrochloric acid (b) Nitric acid (c) Sulphuric acid (d) Acetic acid

943. When safety standards fall, hazards accompany the benefits of modern industrialization. The Bhopal gas tragedy of 1984 in India was caused by the leakage of the heavy, poisonous gas:
(a) Carbon monoxide (b) Methyl isocyanate (c) Phosgene (d) Nerve gas

944. When a small paddle wheel is placed in the path of cathode rays produced under

high vacuum, it starts rotating. This shows that cathode rays are made of:
(a) Waves (b) Ultraviolet light (c) Matter (d) Open space

945. We cannot see the oxygen that we breathe. It is freely available in the air, from which it is obtained for industrial purposes by liquefying it. Liquid oxygen:
(a) Is invisible, like oxygen in the air (b) Looks like water (c) Is blue in colour (d) Is opaque

946. Cast iron is hard and brittle because it contains:
(a) More than 2% carbon (b) More than 1% carbon (c) 5% lead (d) 2 calories of heat

947. Fermentation, a biological process, was thought to be possible only in living organisms. Leading biochemical research showed that fermentation was possible without using cells from living matter. For this contribution to the progress and development of scientific ideas, a Nobel Prize was awarded in 1907 to:
(a) Grignard of France (b) Seaborg of U.S.A. (c) E. Buchner of U.S.A. (d) Todd of Great Britain

948. Beautiful, lake colours are formed by dyes with mordants, which fasten the dye to the cloth or fabric. Which of the following is a mordant used in dyeing?

(a) Calcium hydroxide (b) Aluminium sulphate (c) Calcium carbonate (d) Zinc phosphate

949. When sunlight is split, we get a spectrum of colours, with some dark lines in between. These dark lines tell us which:
(a) Elements of matter are absent in the sun (b) Elements of matter are present in the sun (c) Is the coldest part of the sun (d) Planet is the cause of a solar eclipse

950. The quality of a textile polymer fibre is judged in many ways, some of which are mentioned here. Can you pick the false one?
(a) Resistance to wrinkles (b) Resistance to ageing in the light of the sun (c) Ability to change on heating (d) Ability to withstand washing

951. Which of the following is a yellow-coloured chemical used as a pigment?
(a) Zinc carbonate (b) Zinc oxide (c) Zinc chromate (d) Copper sulphate

952. Some children grow up to be very tall, others remain short, even dwarfs. Tiny amounts of a chemical substance in the body are responsible for these extreme effects. What is it?
(a) A protein (b) An hormone (c) A sugar (d) An enzyme

953. Put water glass and an equal quantity of water in a jar. Then, add salts like sulphates of iron or copper and alum. Crystals of these salts will sink to the bottom and will send up shoots, creating a beautiful:
(a) Money plant (b) Silicon jungle
(c) Colour rainbow (d) Ring of rock crystals

954. Semiconductors are used in transistors. They have bands of energy. Electrons at lower energy level can be excited to these bands at higher energy levels. Which of the following is a common semiconductor material?
(a) Iron (b) Germanium (c) Carbon
(d) Nickel

955. As the fuel crisis deepens, we are looking for alternative sources of energy, some of which are mentioned here. Can you pick the false one?
(a) Solar energy (b) Nuclear fusion
(c) Nuclear fission (d) Tidal power

956. Platinum is a rare, precious metal known for its beauty and quality in jewellery. Platinum that is sold actually, contains six elements mentioned here. Can you pick the false one?
(a) Platinum and Palladium (b) Iridium and Osmium (c) Rhodium and Osmium
(d) Chromium and Rhenium

957. The Crab Nebula can be seen in the sky with a telescope. It is the remnant of a

supernova (a giant star) explosion. At the centre is a pulsar. If a pin is made from the matter of the pulsar, it would weigh:
(a) Only a few micrograms (b) 50 grams
(c) 1.5 tonnes (d) Millions of tonnes

958. A variety of abrasive-coated papers are made for different uses. Which of the following is not an abrasive paper?
(a) Silicon carbide paper (b) Emery paper
(c) Kraft paper (d) Flint paper

959. Heating wood or coal in the absence of air, yields many products some of which are mentioned here. Can you pick the false one?
(a) Coal tar for roads (b) Naphthalene for protecting clothes from moths and insects
(c) Benzene a solvent (d) Wax for candles

960. Permanent magnets can be made from alloys of:
(a) Cobalt (b) Aluminium (c) Zinc (d) Lead

961. Alcohol is used for making some compounds mentioned here. Can you pick the false one?
(a) Chloral (b) Acetaldehyde (c) Benzene
(d) Chlorofrom

962. Scientific reasoning at its heighest reaches, finds it difficult to distinguish matter from energy and energy from matter. Light, a well-known form of energy from sources

like the sun, electric lights and electric heaters, is treated as a form of matter, by saying that it consists of:
(a) Photons or bundles of energy
(b) Electrons or a wave-like matter
(c) Neutrons, since it is electrically neutral
(d) Optical illusions

963. Which of the following is a chemical compound?
(a) Oxygen (b) Iron (c) Salt (d) Diamond

964. An excess of molybdenum in grassy areas results in poor growth of animals because it blocks the ulitization of:
(a) Copper (b) Iron (c) Oxygen
(d) Selenium

965. Iron, a biological nutrient, is found in the human body in:
(a) The protein of hair (b) Haemoglobin of blood (c) The thick bones (d) The hormone adrenaline

966. If a person is injured by the shot of a gun and all the pellets are not removed, it may cause poisoning by:
(a) Mercury (b) Copper (c) Lead (d) Iron

967. It is dangerous to leave the engine of a car running in a closed garage as it may lead to poisoning by:
(a) Carbon dioxide (b) Petrol vapour
(c) Carbon (d) Carbon monoxide

968. Oxygen is abundantly distributed on our planet, either free, or in combination with other elements. Which of the following is incorrect?

(a) Oceans contain 88.9% oxygen (b) Air contains 70% oxygen (c) Sand on deserts and beaches contains 53% oxygen (d) The human body contains 65% oxygen

969. It is said that eating many seeds of apples can cause poisoning in human beings because these seeds contain some amount of:

(a) Sulphur (b) Cyanide (c) Chloride (d) Malic acid

970. Attempts were made in the nineteenth century to find a drug, which when given to the patient, destroyed the germs but did not harm the patient. Such a drug, which combatted diseases like pneumonia and meningitis:

(a) Was trypan red (b) Were the sulphonamides (c) Was carbolic acid (d) Was acetylsalicylic acid

971. One should never touch liquid nitrogen or liquid oxygen because your finger or hand will:

(a) Become yellow (b) Vapourise (c) Crack and finish (d) Disappear

972. Alizarin can be used as a mordant dye in the ways mentioned here. Can you pick the false one?

(a) Cotton dyeing (b) Printing (c) Painting
(d) Chromium lakes for wood dyeing

973. A deadly chemical used in the First World War was a gas that hydrolysed in the lungs to form hydrochloric acid, that ultimately led to suffocation. Which was this chemical weapon?
(a) Ammonia (b) Phosgene (c) Chlorine
(d) Sulphur dioxide

974. One piece of iron metal can attract another by magnetising it. This magnetic property of iron is observed at cold temperatures as well as at hot temperatures. At what temperature does iron cease to behave like a magnet?
(a) 1529°C (b) 768°C (c) 605°C (d) 204°C

975. The word sulphur comes from the Sanskrit word shulbari which means:
(a) Enemy of copper (b) Friend of barium
(c) Bigger than a shawl (d) Burns with iron

976. Plants have a preference for potassium over sodium, even when there is more sodium in the soil. Potassium fertilizers are necessary because on an average, crops take up from the soil:
(a) Half a kilogram (of potassium) per square mile (b) 10 kg of potassium per square kilometre (c) 15 kg of potassium per hectare (d) 25 kg of potassium per acre

977. Silica glass is used in certain specialized optical plates and lenses because ultra-violet light:
(a) Is reflected by it better than by ordinary light (b) Passes through it better than through ordinary glass (c) Is absorbed completely (d) Is converted into visible light

978. A laser is a powerful and accurate beam of light. Some of its applications are mentioned here. Can you pick the false one?
(a) A laser beam can cut steel (b) It can cut a hole as thin as a hair, in diamond (c) It can split water into hydrogen and oxygen (d) It can burn and remove un-wanted flesh during surgery

979. Glass does not react with most acids. However, it does react with:
(a) Hydrofluoric acid (b) Nitric acid (c) Sulphuric acid (d) Hydrochloric acid

980. Molybdenum sulphide is extensively used as a solid grease for lubricating the chassis of motor vehicles. It is a solid, yet it appears greasy because it has a chemical structure like:
(a) Sodium chloride (b) The layers of graphite (c) Ice, that is open (d) Diamond that is a three-dimensional lattice

981. The periodic table has elements related to each other, either in vertical columns or in horizontal rows or even in diagonal loca-

tions. Which of the following groups of elements are related to each other in their physical properties and chemical behaviour:

(a) Hydrogen, helium and calcium (b) Potassium, copper and iron (c) Oxygen, sulphur and selenium (d) Mercury, cadmium and tin

982. High grade steels for special purposes are made:

(a) By the Bessemer process (b) By the Open-hearth process (c) In an electric furnace (d) By duplexing

983. Hydrogen gas can be formed by a variety of chemical reactions, some of which are mentioned here. Can you pick the false one?

(a) Adding sodium borohydride to water
(b) Action of water on calcium hydride
(c) Action of water on sodium amalgam
(d) Action of water on methane

984. An image is formed on a photographic film when a single photon of light strikes it and creates a tiny nucleus (centre) of silver atoms which we cannot see. In order to see, this nucleus has to be developed (enlarged) to a visible size by making it a billion times bigger. What is the minimum number of silver atoms required by each nucleus to allow it to be developed?

(a) 2 (b) 3 (c) 4 (d) 7 million

985. Sulphuric acid is an useful chemical widely used in many industries. The largest use of sulphuric acid is in the manufacture of:
(a) Dyes (b) Drugs (c) Textiles (d) Fertilizers

986. While driving a motor car through busy traffic lanes and crowded places, the gears are often changed, which makes them worn out. To prevent the wear and tear of gears, the gear teeth are heated with potassium cyanide, whereby nitrogen atoms enter the spaces between the iron atoms of the gear and harden it. This process is called:
(a) Galvanization (b) Hard-plating
(c) Case-hardening (d) Alloying

987. When a liquid is heated, it expands in volume. Which gas in cold, liquid form expands when it is further cooled?
(a) Liquid ammonia (b) Liquid helium
(c) Liquid hydrogen (d) Liquid oxygen

988. Many industries were discharging their effluent waste in the River Thames (Great Britain). This increased the temperature of the river and led to a decrease of oxygen in the river. A change like this greatly affects or destroys plants, fishes and other forms of aquatic life. It is known as:
(a) Oxygen decline (b) Water shield
(c) Thermal pollution (d) The temperature effect

989. Rain water sometimes contains ammonium nitrate because lightning in the sky causes the air to react and produce oxides of nitrogen and:
(a) Hydrogen (b) Rare gases (c) Ammonia (d) Carbon dioxide

990. It is generally difficult to make metals into powders. Which metal is powdered, suspended in oil and used as a paint for mirrors?
(a) Iron (b) Aluminium (c) Tin (d) Silver

991. The radioactive property of matter can be used for detecting crime. If a car hits something and runs away, leaving a tiny piece of paint, detectives can tell that the piece belongs to that car, by bombarding a paint sample taken from the car and the fallen piece of paint with neutrons. This will prove that they are identical because of the presence of identical:
(a) Pure brands of paint (b) Impurities in the paint (c) Colour (d) Oil used in the paint

992. Do you know where the word Chemistry comes from? It comes from the word alchemy which comes from:
(a) Cambridge in England (b) Khem the black soil on the Nile (c) Chiming of silver bells (d) The Calm beauty of Pacific Islands

993. Plaster of Paris is used for setting bones and for interior decoration. It is formed

236

by the controlled heating of gypsum, which is a hydrated form of:
(a) Magnesium sulphate (b) Calcium chloride (c) Calcium sulphate (d) Aluminium silicate

994. Aluminium metal is used in many ways. Can you pick the false one?
(a) In making electric wires (b) For making cooking pans (c) For aircraft panels (d) For type-letters in printing work

995. 'Gentlemen, you must learn to dream'. August Kekule saw snakes revolving in his dream. Each snake caught the tail of the other and formed a circle, which led Kekule to a major breakthrough in science. What was his discovery?
(a) The round structure of the planet Mars (b) The spiral arms of a galaxy in the distant sky (c) The round structure of aromatic (sweet-smelling) benzene (d) The nuclear power of uranium

996. Reaching down to very low temperatures by cooling matter is a very difficult task. The path to these low temperatures is approached by magnetizing a substance, cooling it and then:
(a) Passing a current (b) Demagnetising it (c) Allowing it to expand in vacuum (d) Leaving it to stand for seven days

997. Many fuels used in industry are gases or mixtures of gases containing atleast, one

gas which is a carbon compound. Which of the following is incorrect?
(a) Coal gas is made by the destructive distillation of coal (b) Producer gas contains mainly carbon monoxide and nitrogen (c) Methane is made by blowing hot air over coke (d) Water gas is made by blowing steam over hot coke

998. Electric cookers have a coating that protects them against fire. This coating is made of:
(a) Magnesium oxide (b) Heavy lead (c) Zinc oxide (d) Prussian blue

999. Jupiter, the giant planet of the solar system, is more than 300 times bigger than the earth. It was photographed by Pioneer-10, the space probe. Which of the following statements about Jupiter is incorrect?
(a) The darker lower clouds contain sulphur (b) The mantle near the core of Jupiter is magnetic iron (c) The bright bands of Jupiter are high clouds of crystals of ammonia (d) The Great Red Spot is a hurricane (strong wind), 300 years old

1000. The desire to be immortal, that is to live forever, exists in many hearts even today. The coldest place in the world is Verkhoyansk in Siberia where temperatures fall to a chilly depth of -42°C. Further down this frigid scale at the, artificially, created low temperature of -196°C, human life cannot survive. Despite this known fact, some people in the United States have allowed their bodies to be placed in steel drums containing a gas liquefied to —196°C in the hope that science will advance in the far-off future and bring them back to life. Their dead bodies lie preserved in this liquefied gas. Which is this liquefied gas on which precious lives have been gambled for a future unknown?

(a) Liquid ammonia (b) Liquid oxygen
(c) Liquid hydrogen (d) Liquid nitrogen

ANSWERS

1 (b)	2 (c)	3 (b)	4 (d)	5 (a)
6 (b)	7 (c)	8 (c)	9 (c)	10 (d)
11 (b)	12 (c)	13 (b)	14 (c)	15 (d)
16 (c)	17 (b)	18 (d)	19 (b)	20 (d)
21 (c)	22 (b)	23 (d)	24 (a)	25 (b)
26 (a)	27 (a)	28 (c)	29 (b)	30 (b)
31 (c)	32 (b)	33 (c)	34 (d)	35 (a)
36 (b)	37 (b)	38 (d)	39 (c)	40 (b)
41 (a)	42 (b)	43 (a)	44 (d)	45 (b)
46 (d)	47 (d)	48 (a)	49 (b)	50 (c)
51 (b)	52 (a)	53 (d)	54 (a)	55 (b)
56 (a)	57 (d)	58 (c)	59 (c)	60 (b)
61 (c)	62 (b)	63 (c)	64 (c)	65 (b)
66 (c)	67 (b)	68 (b)	69 (a)	70 (d)
71 (c)	72 (b)	73 (d)	74 (b)	75 (d)
76 (b)	77 (c)	78 (a)	79 (d)	80 (c)
81 (d)	82 (b)	83 (b)	84 (c)	85 (b)
86 (d)	87 (c)	88 (c)	89 (d)	90 (c)
91 (c)	92 (a)	93 (d)	94 (a)	95 (a)
96 (b)	97 (a)	98 (b)	99 (a)	100 (b)
101 (d)	102 (a)	103 (b)	104 (b)	105 (c)
106 (c)	107 (b)	108 (c)	109 (d)	110 (a)
111 (c)	112 (c)	113 (b)	114 (c)	115 (d)
116 (c)	117 (b)	118 (c)	119 (c)	120 (a)
121 (b)	122 (c)	123 (d)	124 (b)	125 (b)
126 (b)	127 (d)	128 (a)	129 (b)	130 (d)
131 (c)	132 (c)	133 (b)	134 (d)	135 (b)

136 (c)	137 (b)	138 (c)	139 (d)	140 (c)
141 (b)	142 (c)	143 (b)	144 (d)	145 (c)
146 (b)	147 (c)	148 (c)	149 (a)	150 (d)
151 (c)	152 (d)	153 (c)	154 (d)	155 (b)
156 (a)	157 (a)	158 (b)	159 (b)	160 (c)
161 (c)	162 (d)	163 (d)	164 (c)	165 (b)
166 (c)	167 (b)	168 (c)	169 (a)	170 (b)
171 (b)	172 (a)	173 (d)	174 (c)	175 (c)
176 (c)	177 (d)	178 (c)	179 (c)	180 (b)
181 (c)	182 (b)	183 (d)	184 (b)	185 (c)
186 (c)	187 (a)	188 (d)	189 (c)	190 (d)
191 (a)	192 (b)	193 (c)	194 (d)	195 (a)
196 (b)	197 (c)	198 (c)	199 (c)	200 (a)
201 (a)	202 (b)	203 (a)	204 (b)	205 (c)
206 (b)	207 (a)	208 (b)	209 (b)	210 (d)
211 (d)	212 (b)	213 (a)	214 (b)	215 (d)
216 (d)	217 (b)	218 (d)	219 (b)	220 (c)
221 (d)	222 (d)	223 (a)	224 (c)	225 (b)
226 (d)	227 (a)	228 (d)	229 (b)	230 (d)
231 (b)	232 (c)	233 (c)	234 (c)	235 (c)
236 (b)	237 (c)	238 (a)	239 (a)	240 (b)
241 (a)	242 (b)	243 (a)	244 (b)	245 (c)
246 (a)	247 (b)	248 (d)	249 (b)	250 (c)
251 (c)	252 (d)	253 (c)	254 (c)	255 (a)
256 (b)	257 (b)	258 (d)	259 (b)	260 (c)
261 (c)	262 (b)	263 (a)	264 (c)	265 (a)
266 (c)	267 (a)	268 (b)	269 (c)	270 (d)
271 (d)	272 (a)	273 (b)	274 (a)	275 (d)

276 (b)	277 (c)	278 (c)	279 (d)	280 (c)
281 (a)	282 (b)	283 (b)	284 (d)	285 (c)
286 (d)	287 (b)	288 (d)	289 (c)	290 (d)
291 (b)	292 (d)	293 (c)	294 (c)	295 (b)
296 (c)	297 (c)	298 (b)	299 (c)	300 (d)
301 (d)	302 (a)	303 (b)	304 (b)	305 (b)
306 (c)	307 (a)	308 (b)	309 (b)	310 (c)
311 (b)	312 (d)	313 (a)	314 (a)	315 (c)
316 (c)	317 (b)	318 (c)	319 (d)	320 (a)
321 (b)	322 (d)	323 (c)	324 (b)	325 (a)
326 (b)	327 (b)	328 (c)	329 (c)	330 (b)
331 (c)	332 (d)	333 (b)	334 (c)	335 (d)
336 (b)	337 (b)	338 (c)	339 (b)	340 (b)
341 (c)	342 (c)	343 (a)	344 (c)	345 (b)
346 (b)	347 (c)	348 (a)	349 (d)	350 (c)
351 (c)	352 (c)	353 (c)	354 (a)	355 (b)
356 (b)	357 (a)	358 (b)	359 (d)	360 (b)
361 (c)	362 (c)	363 (c)	364 (c)	365 (d)
366 (c)	367 (a)	368 (b)	369 (b)	370 (a)
371 (a)	372 (a)	373 (c)	374 (b)	375 (b)
376 (d)	377 (c)	378 (c)	379 (c)	380 (d)
381 (b)	382 (b)	383 (b)	384 (a)	385 (c)
386 (c)	387 (c)	388 (d)	389 (b)	390 (d)
391 (b)	392 (c)	393 (d)	394 (c)	395 (a)
396 (b)	397 (b)	398 (b)	399 (c)	400 (d)
401 (a)	402 (c)	403 (c)	404 (d)	405 (d)
406 (b)	407 (c)	408 (d)	409 (c)	410 (b)
411 (a)	412 (a)	413 (c)	414 (b)	415 (c)

416 (a)	417 (b)	418 (c)	419 (b)	420 (b)
421 (d)	422 (d)	423 (d)	424 (d)	425 (b)
426 (c)	427 (d)	428 (c)	429 (c)	430 (b)
431 (d)	432 (c)	433 (c)	434 (b)	435 (b)
436 (a)	437 (b)	438 (d)	439 (d)	440 (c)
441 (c)	442 (d)	443 (a)	444 (b)	445 (b)
446 (b)	447 (d)	448 (b)	449 (d)	450 (d)
451 (b)	452 (d)	453 (c)	454 (c)	455 (b)
456 (b)	457 (b)	458 (b)	459 (c)	460 (b)
461 (c)	462 (d)	463 (b)	464 (c)	465 (c)
466 (d)	467 (a)	468 (b)	469 (d)	470 (b)
471 (a)	472 (b)	473 (a)	474 (d)	475 (c)
476 (c)	477 (b)	478 (b)	479 (c)	480 (b)
481 (b)	482 (b)	483 (b)	484 (c)	485 (b)
486 (c)	487 (b)	488 (d)	489 (c)	490 (a)
491 (b)	492 (b)	493 (a)	494 (c)	495 (d)
496 (d)	497 (c)	498 (b)	499 (c)	500 (c)
501 (b)	502 (b)	503 (a)	504 (d)	505 (d)
506 (d)	507 (c)	508 (c)	509 (d)	510 (b)
511 (b)	512 (a)	513 (c)	514 (b)	515 (d)
516 (b)	517 (a)	518 (d)	519 (d)	520 (c)
521 (d)	522 (b)	523 (c)	524 (d)	525 (c)
526 (b)	527 (b)	528 (b)	529 (c)	530 (c)
531 (c)	532 (b)	533 (d)	534 (c)	535 (b)
536 (b)	537 (c)	538 (b)	539 (d)	540 (b)
541 (c)	542 (c)	543 (d)	544 (b)	545 (b)
546 (a)	547 (d)	548 (b)	549 (b)	550 (b)
551 (b)	552 (c)	553 (c)	554 (c)	555 (b)

556 (c)	557 (d)	558 (b)	559 (c)	560 (c)
561 (b)	562 (c)	563 (b)	564 (c)	565 (d)
566 (d)	567 (d)	568 (b)	569 (c)	570 (a)
571 (b)	572 (c)	573 (c)	574 (b)	575 (a)
576 (c)	577 (c)	578 (c)	579 (d)	580 (c)
581 (c)	582 (d)	583 (b)	584 (c)	585 (c)
586 (b)	587 (c)	588 (b)	589 (b)	590 (b)
591 (d)	592 (d)	593 (d)	594 (b)	595 (b)
596 (b)	597 (a)	598 (b)	599 (b)	600 (d)
601 (b)	602 (b)	603 (b)	604 (c)	605 (b)
606 (b)	607 (b)	608 (b)	609 (c)	610 (c)
611 (d)	612 (d)	613 (a)	614 (d)	615 (c)
616 (a)	617 (b)	618 (c)	619 (b)	620 (c)
621 (c)	622 (b)	623 (d)	624 (c)	625 (c)
626 (b)	627 (d)	628 (c)	629 (c)	630 (c)
631 (b)	632 (b)	633 (b)	634 (c)	635 (b)
636 (d)	637 (c)	638 (b)	639 (a)	640 (b)
641 (b)	642 (d)	643 (d)	644 (d)	645 (d)
646 (c)	647 (b)	648 (d)	649 (b)	650 (b)
651 (c)	652 (b)	653 (c)	654 (b)	655 (c)
656 (a)	657 (c)	658 (d)	659 (c)	660 (a)
661 (b)	662 (c)	663 (d)	664 (b)	665 (b)
666 (d)	667 (d)	668 (c)	669 (b)	670 (d)
671 (d)	672 (c)	673 (b)	674 (b)	675 (c)
676 (b)	677 (c)	678 (b)	679 (a)	680 (d)
681 (c)	682 (a)	683 (a)	684 (d)	685 (b)
686 (c)	687 (a)	688 (c)	689 (c)	690 (a)
691 (c)	692 (b)	693 (b)	694 (d)	695 (c)

696 (c)	697 (d)	698 (c)	699 (c)	700 (d)
701 (c)	702 (b)	703 (b)	704 (c)	705 (d)
706 (b)	707 (b)	708 (d)	709 (d)	710 (d)
711 (b)	712 (b)	713 (b)	714 (d)	715 (b)
716 (b)	717 (a)	718 (c)	719 (c)	720 (d)
721 (b)	722 (c)	723 (b)	724 (b)	725 (d)
726 (a)	727 (d)	728 (d)	729 (c)	730 (b)
731 (b)	732 (c)	733 (c)	734 (b)	735 (d)
736 (b)	737 (c)	738 (b)	739 (c)	740 (d)
741 (d)	742 (b)	743 (b)	744 (c)	745 (b)
746 (c)	747 (b)	748 (c)	749 (c)	750 (d)
751 (c)	752 (b)	753 (c)	754 (c)	755 (c)
756 (c)	757 (a)	758 (a)	759 (b)	760 (b)
761 (b)	762 (c)	763 (b)	764 (d)	765 (c)
766 (b)	767 (d)	768 (d)	769 (b)	770 (d)
771 (a)	772 (d)	773 (a)	774 (d)	775 (c)
776 (c)	777 (c)	778 (d)	779 (d)	780 (d)
781 (d)	782 (c)	783 (a)	784 (c)	785 (d)
786 (c)	787 (c)	788 (c)	789 (c)	790 (c)
791 (c)	792 (b)	793 (b)	794 (c)	795 (c)
796 (b)	797 (c)	798 (b)	799 (c)	800 (a)
801 (b)	802 (d)	803 (b)	804 (d)	805 (b)
806 (b)	807 (c)	808 (d)	809 (b)	810 (c)
811 (d)	812 (b)	813 (c)	814 (d)	815 (c)
816 (d)	817 (a)	818 (c)	819 (d)	820 (c)
821 (c)	822 (d)	823 (d)	824 (c)	825 (b)
826 (b)	827 (b)	828 (c)	829 (b)	830 (b)
831 (c)	832 (b)	833 (c)	834 (c)	835 (c)

836 (b)	837 (c)	838 (a)	839 (c)	840 (b)
841 (b)	842 (c)	843 (b)	844 (b)	845 (a)
846 (b)	847 (a)	848 (b)	849 (c)	850 (c)
851 (a)	852 (d)	853 (c)	854 (d)	855 (d)
856 (b)	857 (b)	858 (c)	859 (b)	860 (b)
861 (d)	862 (b)	863 (b)	864 (b)	865 (c)
866 (d)	867 (c)	868 (b)	869 (b)	870 (b)
871 (b)	872 (b)	873 (b)	874 (c)	875 (c)
876 (d)	877 (b)	878 (b)	879 (d)	880 (b)
881 (c)	882 (c)	883 (b)	884 (c)	885 (a)
886 (b)	887 (c)	888 (b)	889 (a)	890 (b)
891 (b)	892 (d)	893 (a)	894 (b)	895 (b)
896 (c)	897 (c)	898 (b)	899 (c)	900 (b)
901 (a)	902 (c)	903 (c)	904 (c)	905 (b)
906 (d)	907 (b)	908 (d)	909 (c)	910 (b)
911 (c)	912 (b)	913 (a)	914 (d)	915 (a)
916 (b)	917 (c)	918 (b)	919 (c)	920 (d)
921 (d)	922 (c)	923 (b)	924 (c)	925 (c)
926 (c)	927 (b)	928 (c)	929 (c)	930 (c)
931 (d)	932 (a)	933 (b)	934 (a)	935 (c)
936 (d)	937 (c)	938 (c)	939 (b)	940 (c)
941 (a)	942 (c)	943 (b)	944 (c)	945 (c)
946 (a)	947 (c)	948 (b)	949 (b)	950 (c)
951 (c)	952 (b)	953 (d)	954 (b)	955 (c)
956 (b)	957 (d)	958 (c)	959 (d)	960 (a)
961 (c)	962 (a)	963 (c)	964 (a)	965 (b)
966 (c)	967 (d)	968 (b)	969 (b)	970 (b)
971 (c)	972 (c)	973 (b)	974 (b)	975 (a)

976 (d)	977 (b)	978 (c)	979 (a)	980 (b)
981 (c)	982 (c)	983 (d)	984 (c)	985 (d)
986 (c)	987 (c)	988 (c)	989 (c)	990 (b)
991 (b)	992 (b)	993 (c)	994 (d)	995 (c)
996 (b)	997 (c)	998 (a)	999 (b)	1000 (d)